THE
FROG

THE
FROG

A TALE OF SEXUAL TORTURE AND DEGRADATION

CLAIRE THOMPSON

BLUE MOON BOOKS
NEW YORK

THE FROG: *A Tale of Sexual Torture and Degradation*

Copyright ©2006 by Claire Thompson

Published by
Blue Moon Books
An Imprint of Avalon Publishing Group, Incorporated
245 West 17th Street, 11th floor
New York, NY 10011-5300

First Blue Moon Books Edition 2006

ISBN-10: 1-56201-519-2
ISBN-13: 987-1-56201-519-0

Printed in Canada
Distributed by Publishers Group West

THE
FROG

Chapter 1

FROG

Jane got the shopping cart with the wobbly wheel. It veered to the right and she had to keep pulling to the left to stay straight in the aisle. Why did that always happen? More importantly, why didn't she get another cart? But she had already chosen this one, and something of her dogged determination in the face of difficulty made her keep it. She was almost done with her shopping anyway. How long did it take to buy the few items she needed? Food didn't interest her; she ate to stay alive, and her choices reflected her lack of enthusiasm—frozen vegetables, a bag of carrots, two cans of peaches, some preformed hamburgers, a plastic bag of buns, a jar of instant coffee and a quart of milk. Plain food for a plain girl.

Now Jane pushed her lank, pale hair back from her forehead with one hand, while she unloaded her cart onto the conveyor belt. A pimply-faced boy rang up her purchases, looking bored, not noticing Jane at all. No one noticed Jane. That's what she thought. She was wrong.

"That's the one, Robert. She's the one." The tall woman gestured by jerking her head in Jane's direction. Robert, not quite as tall as his wife, but large and strong, looked in the direction she pointed.

"The skinny girl? Why her? She looks so, I don't know, boring!"

"Look in her cart. She's definitely buying for one. Lives alone. No ring. No makeup, no hairstyle to speak of. No one to try and impress. Alone, Miss Lonely Hearts. Perfect."

Robert stared a moment longer, and then nodded approvingly, a slow, mean smile spreading on his fleshy face. "Yeah, you're right, babe, as usual. Yeah." They hung back, watching Jane pay for her paltry purchase, watching as she took the two plastic sacks she had packed herself, watching as she carried them out to her car, a Ford Escort with a dented back fender. Abandoning their cart, the pair followed her out into the lot and Robert said, "You're on, Brenda."

Brenda swung her dark auburn hair back, smiled, and headed confidentially toward Jane. As she approached Jane's car, Brenda knit her brow and assumed a troubled expression. When she was close enough she called out, her voice trembling slightly, "Excuse me, ma'am?"

Jane didn't turn around at first as she fumbled with her car key. She was still hoping that whoever it was wasn't talking to her. But Brenda came closer and said, "Um, miss, excuse me?" Jane looked up reluctantly, her mouth pursed uninvitingly.

"Yes?" Jane's voice was cold.

"I'm so sorry to trouble you, ma'am, but my car? It won't start and it does this sometimes? I was hoping maybe if you didn't mind giving me a jump start? My husband will *kill* me if I'm late again. He, um," she bit her lip, and real tears sprang to her eyes as she finished in a whisper, "he drinks and sometimes he gets, well, you know . . ." She trailed off, looking so miserable and embarrassed that Jane suddenly felt horrible for being so rude. She hated strangers approaching her for any reason. But this poor woman was in a jam. That was clear. It wasn't like Jane had anywhere to rush off to. Just her little apartment and a boring night with the T.V.

"I guess I could help you," Jane said, smiling tentatively.

Brenda sighed histrionically with relief and then gushed, "Oh thank you so much! It won't take but a second. My car's over in the next lot. If you wouldn't mind we could ride over together."

Jane looked unsure, but Brenda's eyes filled again. "Oh, well, I guess I could do that," Jane said, and Brenda suppressed a grin. She climbed in next to Jane and directed, "Just in that next lot, around the corner there." With her direction, Jane ended up behind a small building. Brenda's car was the only one in sight. It flashed through Jane's mind for an instant that it was kind of odd that Brenda should have parked in such an out of the way place. Just as she was considering asking Brenda about this, there was a sharp rap on her window. As Jane turned in surprise at the sound, Robert pulled open the driver door.

"Out you go, girlie!" he said, grabbing Jane's arm and roughly hauling her out of the car. Jane was so startled she barely had time to squeal as Robert shoved her into the back seat of an old station wagon, circa 1972, with bald tires and rusted paint. He slid in next to her, still keeping an iron grip on her arm. Brenda grabbed Jane's keys from the ignition, her purse from the floor of the passenger side, and scooted out to take her place in the driver's seat of the old car. It all happened in seconds.

Brenda was already driving out of the parking lot when Jane finally managed to sputter, "What's going on! What is this? My God, let me go!" Her voice was pitched high with fear and confusion.

Brenda laughed and said, "We got you! That's what! We did it, Robert! We got little Miss Lonely Hearts! She fell for it, lock, stock, and barrel! We're almost home free. Go ahead, do it now. Just gotta do the trade off with the car and then the fun begins!"

"You are so right, Brenda. This little cunt is going to work out just fine." He pulled Jane closer to him, still holding her arm in his meaty, strong grip. She tried to wrestle herself free, panic rising in her like an acid balloon, but with his other hand he grabbed the back of her head and pulled her face to his, kissing her roughly on the mouth, forcing his tongue between her teeth, shocking poor Jane into terrified silence. His breath was sharp with stale cigarettes.

Finally, he let her go, forcing her head down onto his lap, so her face was mashed into his zipper. Holding her still with little effort, he laughed and said, "I think she liked that, Brenda! The little frog was just waiting for a prince like me to kiss her!" He laughed loudly at his own joke. Brenda rolled her eyes, but smiled indulgently at her husband. She concentrated on the road, driving carefully so as not attract attention. She was eager to get home so they could play with their new toy.

Still holding down his squirming, squealing charge, Robert got out the chloroform-soaked rag he had prepared for this moment. He had kept it in a zip lock bag, which was waiting at his feet. Holding her by the back of her neck, Robert placed the rag over Jane's nose and mouth, forcing her to breathe in the noxious fumes. After just a few moments, he felt her go limp in his arms.

They pulled in at the abandoned factory on the edge of town. Luck was with them as they parked behind the dilapidated old building. A lone car waited, out of place in the parking lot now overgrown with weeds. Parking the old car next to a new shiny Lexus, Brenda moved from one car to the other. Robert got out and then managed to heft Jane's now limp form out of the car and into the back seat of the second car. If anyone had seen them leave the supermarket parking lot, they would be looking for an old junk heap, not Robert's new model Lexus pride and joy.

Once they were driving again, Robert adjusted Jane so she was lying on his lap, her eyes closed, and a peaceful expression on her face. "She doesn't look as ugly when she's sleeping. I would say from the looks of her that she hasn't been getting any for quite some time! If ever!" Again the cruel laugh. He spoke now to the unconscious woman. "Well, your days of waiting are over, cunt. You have just been selected to be our sex slave, our love tool, our personal piece of ass." With one strong hand he grabbed Jane's blouse and ripped it open, causing the buttons to spray against the soft leather of the car seat. Next, he used his pocketknife to slice through the practical cotton bra that covered Jane's smallish breasts.

He held the silver blade close to her neck, fantasizing for a moment about slicing through the jugular; watching the blood spurt in a stream from her throat. Almost reluctantly, he closed the knife and slipped it in his back pocket. If he killed her now, they would have to find someone new. And anyway, he would never do that to his new Lexus.

Instead, he focused his attention on her chest. "Ah," he said, as he stared at her naked torso, the little nipples a dark pink against white skin. He could see pale blue veins through her porcelain flesh. Brenda glanced in the rearview mirror at the scene in the back seat. She drove faster, wanting to get home quickly so she could join in the fun.

Robert, with Jane's head still resting on his lap, lifted himself to unzip his jeans. Using one hand, he pulled his large, thick cock out of his pants. He wasn't wearing any underwear so it was easy to do, and he sighed with relief since his erection had been getting painful in anticipation over how they would use this piece of ass they had stolen.

Slowly he began to massage his massive cock, licking his lips as he stared down at the unconscious woman. "You did good this time, Brenda. We are gonna have some serious fun with this one." Brenda smiled, eyes on the road. She would do anything to keep her man happy. Not that she didn't enjoy the game as well. For her the thrill was in the abduction. Finding the target, honing in, making the escape without getting caught. Even now, when they were almost home free, her heart was racing with adrenaline.

And when they got her home, safe in their compound, Brenda's pleasure would center around the control; the torture. Yes, she liked the sex, but that was primarily Robert's domain. He was insatiable and she adored him. If that meant handing over little pieces of ass for him to use and abuse, Brenda was more than happy to oblige. As long as they weren't too pretty. This one would do just fine.

She glanced again in the rearview mirror. Robert was staring down at Jane, pumping himself hard, his mouth open, his tongue out. After a few more minutes he moaned and yelled, "Yes!" as he came, spurting the jism on her face and breasts. Sighing happily, he left his sperm to dry in her hair and on her face and clothing as they finished the ride home. Jane began to stir and Robert quickly held the poisoned rag over her face until she stilled. The next half hour passed quietly, though the air was electric with anticipation.

Jane was still out when they pulled into the long, winding private drive to their house, which was set at least a quarter mile from the main road. They had it built for privacy, including a twelve foot electrified fence that surrounded the five acre property. It prevented anyone from getting in without an invitation— or out.

Robert carried the lifeless Jane effortlessly in his arms. She barely weighed more than a child, it seemed to him. But her tits were okay, not huge, but definitely nice tits. He liked tits. He liked to do all sorts of wonderful horrible things to tits. Jane would learn all about that. He smiled, actually drooling slightly at the thought of what he was going to do to this new piece of ass, this cunt, this little frog. That's what he would call her. Frog. She looked like one, with her rather broad, flat features, and her long skinny legs. And he was her prince. Lucky bitch.

Brenda led the way, opening the door they rarely even bothered to lock. The electric fence and neighborhood security guards were ample protection. Robert followed, carrying Jane in his arms. They entered the large living room, which was two steps down and opened into a wide sunny room with skylights strategically placed to let in light at all times of the day. It was a pretty room, decorated in soft yellows and earth tones. Neither Brenda nor Robert had an eye for such things, but they had let the decorator do as she wished and were happy with the results.

Robert dumped Jane onto the double-sized soft leather couch. He sat down next to her, gauging that the chloroform should be wearing off any time now. After several more minutes, Jane stirred, slowly opening her eyes. She moaned, disoriented. Her head hurt and there was a terrible metallic taste in her mouth. As her vision cleared, she saw Robert looming over her. Jerking upright, she screamed, covering her chest with her hands, trying to back away. Her cry was cut off by Robert's hand over her mouth. "Shut up, frog!" His voice was loud as he clamped his hand hard over her mouth. Jane began to tremble again, and tears filled her eyes, which were big as plates.

"Now listen, cunt. If I take my hand off, you better fucking be quiet, okay? Otherwise, I'll cut that little tongue right out! I can't stand all that squealing and shit. That is, unless I'm the one making you squeal."

He shouldn't have said that, because poor Jane's eyes rolled back and she went limp against the couch. Robert noticed with disgust that she'd wet herself. "Jesus," he swore, "Good thing that couch's leather!" as Brenda came to stand beside him.

"Robert, you're scaring the piss out of her, literally! Ease up, man. Look, why don't you go get us some lunch, and I'll deal with her for a while, okay? Let's not give her a fucking heart attack before we've even gotten to have any fun! Okay?"

"Yeah, okay, whatever," Robert grumbled, but he listened to

Brenda, as he usually did. Brenda looked down on the poor woman, on the disheveled, lank hair, now sticky with cum, her ripped blouse and the blue jeans stained with fear. Almost as strong as Robert, Brenda leaned down and lifted the thin young woman into her arms, carrying her into the small room that would become Jane's bedroom, or more accurately, her prison.

There was no bed in the room, but rather a large cage with thick metal bars at two-inch intervals. It had some old blankets inside of it, and would hold an adult if that person curled up or lay on their side. A large water bottle was secured to the side, with a little metal straw hanging down, like in an animal cage. On the walls of the room were various hooks and manacles, placed to secure a person against the wall at varying heights and angles. There was one small window high in a corner, through which a blood-red sun was setting.

The room wasn't large. In the corner opposite the cage newspapers were spread, as if indeed an animal would be staying here. Near the newspapers a small drain had been set into the floor. Pulleys and hooks were embedded in the ceiling, and hooks were set here and there in the floor. The floor was actually slanted slightly, toward the drain. This way they could hose down their prisoners without flooding the house. Chains and rope were neatly coiled and hung on hooks too high to reach without a ladder. There was no furniture in the room.

The cage door was open, and Brenda set Jane down inside of it and then quickly secured the latch, locking it with a key she kept round her neck. Reaching up to a small video camera in the corner of the room, she removed a protective lens and then smiled for the camera, as if posing for a picture. Taking a last glance at the still unconscious Jane, she left the room to join Robert for lunch.

When Jane awoke again she was first aware of her pounding head and that sickly sweet metallic taste in her mouth. When she tried to move; to stretch out and assess any damage, she found that she was cramped. She tried to sit up, but realized she couldn't. She was in some kind of cage! As she came fully, painfully awake, she realized she had wet her pants, and it all came rushing back to her. The terrifying situation hit her with a force that would have knocked her down if she'd been standing. She lay still for some minutes, trying to control her rapid breathing; trying to assess the situation.

Moving carefully, Jane flexed various limbs to determine if there was any damage. She seemed to be all right, at least physically. She remembered the abduction and the horrible car ride with the large horrible man who had frightened and hurt her. She remembered the sickening nausea, the blackening of her sight, the ringing in her ears as she had passed out. And coming to again with the big man looming over her. That time she welcomed the escape of the darkness as she fell back into a false and short-lived peace. If only she could go back there, escape back to oblivion.

At least no bones were broken. She was in one piece and she was alive, if captive. There must be some way out of this! She willed herself to calm down and slow her breathing. If she could just think. But her head was clouded with fear and confusion.

She moved slightly, uncomfortable in her wet jeans, too frightened to be embarrassed, shifting her weight as she tried to see where she was. Track lighting along the edges of the ceiling lit the room. She would learn that these lights never dimmed. She was always to be visible; always on display. As she took in the instruments of torture, the ropes and chains, the manacles, she drew in her breath audibly. These people weren't just kidnappers. They were insane! They were going to kill her in some horrible, painful way. She started to cry, great noisy gulping sobs of fear.

In the kitchen, Robert and Brenda were eating sandwiches. They heard Jane's cries from the microphones hidden in her room. Their eyes turned quickly to the large screen which projected the video image of Jane's room, with her cage the main focus. "Looks like she's up," Brenda noted, her mouth still full of meat and bread.

She swallowed, took a noisy slurp of beer and then continued, "Let's let her stew awhile. We can finish lunch and then see how our new pussy is doing." Robert grinned broadly and stared up at the screen. Jane's cries had subsided to snuffled sobs, her head hidden in her arms.

About twenty minutes later the pair entered the room and Jane's head jerked up. She regarded them fearfully, but her mouth was too dry with terror to speak. "Hi, froggy," Robert said good naturedly, as if greeting a little niece or an old friend. "How ya like your new digs? Had it refurbished especially for you. Like new. Hope you like it, because you'll be staying there a while. In fact, quite a while. Unless, that is," he paused dramatically, knowing he had her full attention, "Unless you don't cooperate. Fully. Then you'll be out of here in a cocaine heartbeat. *If* you know what I mean."

Jane paled. She was sure she knew what he meant. She listened to him now as if her life depended on it. "Now, you do everything we ask and you stay alive. You do it *well* and you slowly earn privileges. Little things, like food and water. You fuck up, and oh boy, are you gonna pay."

Jane looked at him blankly. She seemed to have no idea what he was saying. Brenda said, "Here's the thing, Jane." Jane's eyes opened even wider, and Brenda, responding to her unspoken question, said, "Sure we know you're name. We have your purse. What'd you think, we'd leave it behind for the police? No one's gonna find you. Ever. You belong to us now. Our slave girl. You see," she said, kneeling down beside the shaking woman, "We have stolen you, and we plan to keep you. Forget about your past life, Janie girl.

"From now on you exist solely to please us. To entertain us.

And we have kind of, uh, shall we say, bizarre tastes. As you might have guessed from the room here."

"Please," Jane managed to whisper.

"She speaks!" Robert observed.

"Please," she tried again, "please let me go. I'll get you money. I can get money." This was a lie, but now hardly seemed the time to be truthful.

"We don't need your money, frog," Robert said disdainfully. I don't guess you got to notice where you are, but we are what you would call independently wealthy. Brenda's dad made his money in oil, and then had the bad luck to drop dead of a heart attack, leaving everything he owned to dear little Brenda here. We've got all the money we need, honey girl. In fact, we're too fucking rich, and it's made us bored. That's why we need a distraction. A toy. A girl toy to play with. In a word, you."

"Please," Jane began again, but Brenda cut her off.

"That's enough. Stop talking. We don't want to hear it. You're still in shock. You'll figure it out soon. Now, as Robert was telling you before, we have house rules. You start out with nothing. You are a slave. Scum of the earth. Shit. Slowly you can earn your way into our graces. We will set tasks for you, and you do them. You do them well and you are rewarded. You do them poorly, and you are punished. Am I clear?"

Jane only stared at her. Brenda continued, "That was your first transgression. You need to learn from the outset that the first rule here is speak when spoken to, and otherwise shut up. We don't want to hear your opinions on anything, unless of course we ask. Then we expect an honest and immediate answer. First transgression equals first punishment. And ignorance is no excuse. You will never say you didn't know a rule and that's why you broke it. You break it, you pay the price. Period. So your first punishment is no food or water until we say so."

Robert looked impatient. He was less interested in control; in mind games. That was Brenda's forte. He liked sensation. Physical, visceral thrills. He liked to hear them scream. He shifted from one foot to the other, like a little boy waiting for permission to be excused. Brenda turned toward him, smiling indulgently. "Go ahead, I know you can't wait. What's on your list for the frog's first day?"

Robert licked his lips and smiled cruelly. "Janie Frog. You wet your pants. You're disgusting. Take off those wet pants and those nasty panties. Now. From in there. Move it."

Jane was too terrified to argue. She clung to a thread that if she obeyed them they might let her go after a while. After all, what other hope had she? With hands trembling so hard she could barely get her fingers to bend, Jane managed to unbutton her jeans and slide the zipper down. She was contorted on her side, trying to pull the wet pants from her body. Even with the fear of imminent death, she managed to blush fiercely at the knowledge that they were watching her pull down her jeans. She finally got them off. Robert knelt down and unlatched the cage, indicating that Jane should push the pants out. She did so.

"Good girl. Now the panties."

"Oh, God," Jane whispered, pleading in her voice.

"Do it, bitch," Brenda ordered, and something in her tone brooked no resistance. Miserably, Jane pulled off her wet panties and tossed them through the cage door.

Robert reached in now and grabbed Jane's arm, pulling her roughly out of the cage. He pulled her up so she was standing, bare assed, her ripped blouse and cut bra useless. She tried to cover her pubic area with one hand while holding her shirt together with the other, but Brenda came up behind her and pulled back her arms, pinning them behind her back. Jane screamed in pain and surprise as Brenda wrenched them up and back.

Robert stood in front of her, appraising the skinny girl, admiring the lush dark blonde pubic curls. He leaned down, his face close to her mons and then said, his voice dripping with disgust, "You stink! Old piss! What a pig!" Laughing cruelly, he nodded at Brenda, who used one foot to kick Jane's legs far apart. She held Jane tight so she couldn't fall. Robert reached down and pressed a large beefy finger into Jane's pussy. Jane screamed again.

"This is getting tedious, Robert. Do something about her screaming, for Christ's sake." Robert picked up Jane's urine-soaked panties and forced them into Jane's mouth. She spluttered and tried to pull back, horrified, but she only managed to press into Brenda who advised, "Better bite down and shut up, girlie, or you'll really be sorry."

Jane believed her. She bit down on the wet fabric, sobs choking in her throat. Meanwhile, Robert continued to finger fuck her. "This bitch is one tight little cunt, Bren. I wouldn't be surprised if she never got any! Who would want her, anyway? Skinny, pale little thing. Not worth fucking, is she? Well, never mind. We can do lots and lots of fun things to get her fuckable."

"Let's chain her up and mark her. I like my slaves marked right away, you know, Robert." As Brenda spoke, she forced Jane over to the wall pressing against her neck so Jane's cheek was mashed against the cold wall. Deftly she placed Jane's wrists into manacles set in the wall, which she adjusted so that Jane was forced onto her tiptoes. Taking a long scarf, she tied it across Jane's face, forcing the wet panties further into the poor woman's mouth.

Robert brought his wife the cane, a long rod of bamboo, bound in black leather with a bright red painted tip. Brenda whooshed it through the air and said to Jane, "Your ass is next." Then she let the cane land, slicing flesh, raising a welt on Jane's small bottom and eliciting a muffled cry of agony from the bound girl. Expertly, Brenda wielded the cane, lashing each cheek several times till there was an angry crisscross of red welts on her ass and thighs.

Robert loved to watch his wife torturing someone. It got him so hot he had to unzip his pants and pull his cock out again, massaging it lovingly as Brenda beat Jane. "Her ass must be so hot, Bren. Do you think . . . ?" He didn't finish the question, but Brenda knew what he was asking.

"Go ahead. Fuck that bony little ass, if that's what turns you on, lover. Why not? Just grease it up or you're gonna have trouble with her puny little butt."

Robert nodded, quickly getting the tube of lubricant they kept handy for such occasions. He smeared it on his cock and pressed his hand between Jane's butt cheeks, smearing a glob on her little asshole. Jane was slumped in her manacles, her wrists bearing most of her weight. She was still quiet, and it wasn't clear if she was conscious or not, but Robert didn't care. He just wanted to fuck her nasty little asshole.

Pressing against her, his pants tight around his muscular thighs, Robert put the tip of his cock against her gooey hole. He pressed, gently at first, then harder, forcing himself into her. Jane jerked and screamed into her gag. Her ass felt like it was being split in two. His rough jeans scraped against her bruised and welted skin. Jane writhed in agony, her piercing screams muffled against her gag.

"She's so hot," Robert moaned, aroused by her obvious terror and pain. He eased in slowly, but relentlessly, pushing his way past her tight sphincter. And then he was fucking the hapless woman, rutting into her, using her like a dog. It only lasted a few minutes, because his arousal and need were so great. With a loud groan of pleasure, Robert shot his thick wad of cum into Jane's ass. He pulled out, wiping his cock with the cloth Brenda handed him.

"Got any left for me?" Brenda asked, smiling coquettishly at her husband. Robert turned to his wife, who had unbuttoned her blouse, revealing her own large breasts and erect nipples. Robert grinned and they left the room to have sex together, both wildly excited by what they had done. For the moment Jane was forgotten, or at least not necessary. It was as if the manacled half-naked woman, with the welted, bruised ass and semen dripping from her asshole was nothing more than an object. Not a real human, but a toy that existed solely to titillate and amuse its owners. And this was only the beginning.

Chapter 2

PRISONER

When Brenda finally came back an hour later to let Jane down, she admired her handiwork. Jane was quiet, her eyes closed, body toward the wall where she still was bound. The scarf was still wound around her head, holding the soiled panties in her mouth. Her ass was bruised and long red lines marked her buttocks and thighs. Robert's semen had dried in a long thin line down her thigh.

Jane jumped when Brenda came up quietly behind her and cupped her naked, welted ass. She moaned slightly behind the gag. "Poor baby," Brenda crooned. "You must be awful tired chained up there, huh girlie? If I let you down, are you gonna be a good little girl?" Jane didn't move and Brenda, was concerned for a second they'd overdone it for her first day. It didn't do to scare them so bad they lost their minds. More fun to keep them lucid; aware of what was happening to them. For Brenda, it wasn't just about physical thrills. She liked to take a person and slowly break them down. Take an independent, functioning adult and reduce them to a docile, totally submissive and obedient slave. Robert could use her, but ultimately it was Brenda who would own her.

"Jane," she whispered, close to the young woman's ear. "Can you hear me? Nod if you can hear me, and I'll let you down. You've done very well for your first day, and I'm going to let you have some water now, if you behave. Would you like that?" Jane was in fact conscious, though her body felt paralyzed from being bound for so long. She stayed very still, like a cornered animal. Perhaps if she didn't move, she wouldn't be caught, her unconscious mind told her. But the mention of water made Jane realize she was gaspingly, achingly thirsty. Her tongue was stuck to the damp fabric of her panties and her throat felt filled with bitter sawdust. Slowly she nodded her head, desperate for water.

"Good girl," Brenda smiled behind her, relieved. Jane could take it. That was good. They would find just how much she could take, and give it to her good. She released the catches on the manacles and was ready when Jane slumped down. Brenda caught her and eased her to the ground. She untied the scarf and pulled the panties from Jane's stiff jaws. Gently, she slipped a straw between Jane's lips. Jane gratefully sipped the cool liquid. Nothing had ever tasted so good to her. Brenda allowed her to finish the glass. Then she cradled Jane's head in her lap.

"I know you haven't taken it all in, but don't worry, you have plenty of time. This is your new home. See that newspaper over there? That's your toilet. You'll relieve yourself there. You can pee in the drain there. You'll get a shower when we feel like hosing you down. Slaves don't use bathrooms in this house. As you may have noticed, Robert likes sex, and his tastes are eccentric." Brenda smiled at her own understatement. "I like control. I will teach you how to behave. How to submit. How to suffer. You start at the bottom. You are nothing more than an animal. A little piggy. Or frog, as Robert seems to like to refer to you. I don't want to hear you complaining. I don't want to hear you begging to be set free or any of that shit. You start whining or trying any of that, and I'll make you wish you'd never been born. Is that clear?"

Jane nodded, trying to stay still, too exhausted to even consider protest. "Good," Brenda said. "Now let's take off that ugly little blouse." As she spoke, she pulled the useless garment from Jane's thin shoulders. Jane's B-cup bra, once white, was an old gray, stained from too many washings. Brenda pulled the torn pieces and tossed them aside. Jane was totally naked now. Brenda held her thin wrists easily in one hand.

A dull red blush suffused Jane's features as Brenda critically examined her small but pretty breasts. They were high and firm and the nipples were a dusty pink. "Pretty," Brenda admitted grudgingly. "Really the only pretty thing about you. You are one plain Jane, aren't you?" she remarked with casual cruelty. Jane turned her head, the remark stinging, a sharp familiar slap that took her back to high school, when heartless popular girls had made much the same comments behind their hands in the lunchroom, in the locker room, or at the occasional dance Jane was stupid enough to attend, just loud enough for her to overhear.

Brenda stood up and left Jane lying on the floor. "I like rope," she said cryptically. Jane closed her eyes and thought she must have misheard as Brenda said, "Want some ice cream, baby?" The woman was insane, Jane decided. She didn't make sense. But Brenda asked again. "I've got mango sherbet or chocolate fudge ripple. You can pick. I'll tie you up and then I'll feed you. I like to do that. Make my slave all helpless and then feed her. Like a baby. You wanna be my baby, sugar?" Brenda was speaking in a high singsong voice; the voice of a mother to her child. Jane's blood curdled with fear. This was worse than someone just killing her outright.

Jane choked back her rising desire to scream. She felt it welling up inside of her like a bubble, ready to burst from her. But maybe if she played the game; appeared to be cooperating, maybe that would at least buy her some time until she could figure a way out of this nightmarish ordeal.

"Mango, please," she managed to whisper. Brenda grinned.

"Excellent choice, froggy. I'll just get you all snug-like and then I'll bring your dessert." Brenda hummed tunelessly under her breath as she busied herself with the ropes. She unwound the white thin cording and kneeling down, rolled Jane onto her side. Pulling Jane's arms behind her, Brenda bound her at the elbows, wrapping the rope down to the wrists, forcing her to arch her back. She pulled her to her feet, so that Jane's breasts were thrust up and out, like a pretty offering.

"Very nice." She stood back a moment, admiring the trussed young woman. "Robert!" she called. "Your frog isn't a total loss. Come check out these tits!" A minute later Robert came lumbering into the room, yawning. He had pulled on his jeans, but remained shirtless, his massive hairy chest exposed. He eyed the young girl appreciatively.

"Nice boobs," he said. "Boy am I gonna have some fun with those!" Jane's head was down, her eyes closed. Brenda pushed her down to her knees, and then caught her as she lost her balance, falling again to her side. Robert knelt down beside her, bringing his mouth down to one succulent breast. He bit the nipple gently, causing Jane to gasp. His long tongue swirled against her, and the nipple went erect. "That's it," he said, and bent forward to bite and lick the other nipple.

Jane felt faint. Her ass was stinging from the beating and her asshole was sore and tender. Her arms hurt from being pulled back so far behind her. In spite of all this, somehow his mouth on her nipples awoke some tiny breath of desire in her loins. She would never have admitted it, but what he did felt good. Not that she could focus on it very well, as uncomfortable as she was. "Tie her tits, Brenda." Brenda nodded. Expertly she wound loops of rope around the base of each breast, cutting off the blood flow, pushing them up hard, with pointed tips.

Jane was mewling, little plaintive cries of fear. Robert leaned toward her and slapped one breast, hard. Jane screamed and tried in vain to wriggle away. He slapped the other one, eliciting another cry of pain and fear from the bound woman, as she jerked hard.

"Okay, okay, Robbie. That's enough. I promised our little girl some sherbet for her reward. You can wait here, but ease up a little. Don't forget it's her first day. We have plenty of time to teach her the ropes." She grinned at her own pun and left the room.

Jane was alone with Robert. He sat down on the floor next to her and idly stroked her distended nipples. She couldn't move and didn't dare protest. She closed her eyes instinctively, as if this would somehow protect her from him. Each breast was bunched at the base, making it hard and forcing the nipples out. Robert circled each nipple with his large fingers. Twisting each one until Jane winced, blushing all the while, he said, "You look good enough to eat, baby. Just put a bag over that sour face of yours and you ain't half bad."

He bent down over her and gently bit her right nipple. His teeth closed tighter and Jane gave a frightened squeal. He released her, the nipple now red and shining with his saliva. Taking the other one between his teeth he bit again, this time harder, and Jane screamed.

When Brenda returned with a large crystal goblet filled with rich yellow sherbet, Robert sat back suddenly, like a child caught with his hand in the cookie jar. Jane continued to whimper quietly, but Brenda didn't seem to notice. She took the long-handled silver spoon and dipped it into the cup. Holding it to Jane's mouth she said, "Here you go, sweetie. Open wide."

Jane felt the cold ice cream against her lips and opened her eyes. Brenda pressed gently and Jane parted her lips. The sherbet was homemade, with bits of orange mango and tiny pieces of crushed ice. Jane had never tasted anything so sweet and tart; so absolutely delicious. Somehow pain and fear had heightened all her sensibilities, including her sense of taste. She licked the spoon and felt a second's regret when it was withdrawn.

But it was returned, freshly heaped with another delicious bite. Jane's breasts ached from the tight ropes wound around them. She tried to focus instead on the sherbet, savoring each bite.

"What a good baby you are," Brenda crooned. As she continued to feed Jane, Robert leaned down, licking and suckling at her nipples. A confusion of pain and pleasure flooded through the exhausted woman. She was on the edge of collapse. Brenda fed her the last of the sherbet and then said, "Let's let this poor baby get some rest. She's done pretty good for the first day, don't you agree?"

Robert nodded, watching as Brenda untied Jane's breasts. As the blood flowed back, the nerve endings in Jane's breasts zinged with pain. Tears sprang to her eyes. Robert massaged his cock through his pants. Brenda finished untying the complex knots that held their captive.

"Get in your cage, frog," Brenda commanded, her voice no longer soft and sweet, but hard and brooking no disobedience. "Don't stand up; crawl like the cunt you are." Jane obeyed, frightened anew by the sudden dark change in Brenda's demeanor. They left her there, terrified and alone. At least that, she thought. Alone. And still alive. Still alive! They had left the light on, but Jane was so exhausted that she barely noticed. She moved slightly on the old blankets, seeing the camera in the corner for the first time. She turned her back to it, and tried to cover herself with the blankets. Before she could further contemplate the horror of her situation, Jane fell into a troubled sleep. Exhaustion had overcome fear.

In the morning Robert came in with a tray of food. There was a bagel, some bacon, and a cup of coffee, black. The smell was heavenly and Jane was instantly awake, though she didn't move, afraid to draw his attention. Robert set the tray down and moved toward her cage, unlatching it. "Morning, frog. Here's some food. You'll need your strength today. Eat up and do your business, because you're gonna be awful busy after that." He laughed and then mercifully turned and left the room.

Jane slipped out of her cage. All her muscles ached from sleeping in the uncomfortably close quarters. Her ass was sore but she wasn't really hurt, she realized with relief. And she was still alive. Maybe they didn't plan to kill her. At least not right away. Her heart began thumping with fear again, and Jane made a concerted effort to calm herself. There had to be some way out of this, if she could just think straight. Meanwhile that food! The mango sherbet was just a distant memory to her empty belly. This food smelled so wonderful; Jane never remembered any food ever smelling so good.

Taking one of her blankets, Jane wrapped herself in it like it was a bath towel. She hurried to the tray, determined to eat before they changed their minds and took it away from her.

The coffee was hot and she scalded her mouth a little sipping it too fast. Though she preferred cream and sugar, this coffee was delicious and she savored it. The bagel was fresh and lightly buttered, and Jane reveled in the soft chewy dough, trying to make it last, but ending by stuffing it into her mouth. The bacon was perfectly cooked, not too floppy, not too crispy. Jane had never tasted anything so delicious in her life. All too quickly, the food and coffee were gone, and Jane became aware that she needed to pee.

She looked around the room, staring for a minute at the camera, toying briefly with the idea of trying to cover it up with one of her blankets. Pulling her blanket tighter around her, she knew that she didn't dare.

Instead, she walked over to the drain and squatted tentatively over it, holding the edges of the blanket up as best she could, and turning her back to the camera as much as possible. It took a few moments for her body to relax sufficiently for her to pee, but eventually she did, feeling the relief of emptying her bladder.

Thank God she didn't have to move her bowels yet. She wouldn't even think about that now. Jane looked around for something to wipe herself with, but there was only old newspaper. Reluctantly, she ripped a piece of it and used it, not with great success, to wipe the remaining droplets of urine away. She crumpled the soiled paper and set it in a corner.

Returning to her tray, she inspected it for any missing crumbs. As she was draining any last drops hiding in the coffee cup she heard the key and jumped slightly, her heart at once beginning a pounding rhythm in her chest and throat. The door opened and Brenda came in. "Hi Jane. How'd you sleep? Breakfast all right?"

"Fine," Jane managed to croak, nodding. She hunched down, hugging herself, still wrapped in her blanket. It seemed so incongruous the way they talked to her like she was some kind of guest and then treated her so viciously.

"Let's get something clear from the start here. Slaves and animals don't wear clothes. Drop it. Now!" Jane held the blanket tightly against herself for a few seconds longer. Then she let it go, watching it fall to the floor as she clutched her naked form, the blush moving in a heat down her chest.

"Oh, by the way, I like a little formality, though Robert doesn't care a whit. But you will call me *ma'am,* or *mistress,* or *Miss Brenda.* Never answer, 'fine,' like you did just now, or I'll punish you. Consider yourself warned. Got it, missy?"

"Yes, ma'am," Jane whispered.

"Much better. Now listen, Jane. Today you get a choice. Do you want to be tortured or used?" She paused, looking at Jane. When the girl didn't answer Brenda went on, "You look confused. I'll clarify. Actually both things are going to happen, but today I'm giving you a choice which you want first. By *used* I mean sexually, stupid. By Robert. I'll use you too, but not yet. I'll wait till you're at least a little trained before we focus on *that.* But Robert is a horny little bugger, and he just loves to break in our new fillies. So today you're going to get used, *and* you're going to get tortured. My question is, which do you want first?"

Jane stared at her, dumbfounded. How could she answer? Was this a trick, a test? Would she fail? But it didn't really matter, did it? They would do what they wanted to her and she would endure it because she had no choice. She might have protested. She might have begged; tried to bargain or plead her way out. But Jane was basically a fatalist. A pessimist born of years of setting herself up for failure, or reaching only as far as she dared and never further. As she had so often thought over her short life, "What good would it do anyway?"

Still, at least she could put off the pain a little while longer—the sting of the cane was fresh in her mind. Brenda was looking at her, waiting for an answer. Slowly Jane said, "Used, ma'am."

"Slut," Brenda hissed, feigning disgust. "I knew you were a slut. Robert thinks you're a virgin, but you're just a skanky snatch, aren't you, whore? Answer me!" Brenda sounded angry, though it was mostly an act. She could see that Jane was excruciatingly uncomfortable with her own body. Brenda critically noted her skinny frame and flat little butt with satisfaction. She compared her in her mind to her own voluptuous curves and smiled, her eyes narrowing. Still, there *was* a hint of jealousy behind the words. Robert took so much obvious pleasure from being with other women that sometimes Brenda, as self-confident as she was, felt left out. Fear was the driving force behind her insecurity, fear that her husband would one day leave her, though the lavish style of life she was able to provide for him did give her a sizable edge, she was sure.

Jane was flustered by Brenda's acid response, and not a little afraid. It seemed that this Brenda actually expected some kind of response. "Please, ma'am, I'm not a-a slut," she stumbled over the word.

Brenda cut her off, "Oh yes you are, cunt. Don't contradict me.

You're a slut and cunt whore who is trying to steal my husband. Well, it won't work. But it's good you picked sex first, because then I get the pleasure of punishing you for being such a slut!" Brenda flounced out the door, leaving a horrified Jane to wonder what she had done wrong this time.

Robert came in some minutes later, unaware of the exchange between the two women. He knew Brenda got slightly jealous of his interactions with their toys, but he liked that; kept the old bitch on her toes. In fact, he did love Brenda, and relied on her not just for her money, but for her direction. She was the leader of the two of them, the plan maker, the organizer. She picked their targets and she set things up so Robert could use their toys until they were used up and disposed of.

Robert was excited and happy with their newest acquisition. She was young and terrified and probably not very experienced sexually. He would have the privilege of breaking her in to all sorts of nasty and exciting practices. He would turn her from cold frigid bitch to wanton sex slave. He would teach her not just to submit sexually, but to crave it; to live for it. And despite his very selfish use of their toys, Robert was in fact quite attuned to what drove women wild. He knew how to take them to the edge and pull them back, and then push them closer, closer, controlling their experience until he finally let them go, pushing them toward their own little deaths, leaving them completely spent and, in his mind, properly used.

Today would be frog's first taste of sexual pleasure at Robert's hand. She would have to earn it, of course. Without outwardly acknowledging Jane, who sat in a corner of the room, legs drawn up protectively around her, Robert moved a large but light metal frame into the center of the room. There were Velcro straps placed at intervals to properly secure a person to it.

He turned to her. "Get over here, frog," Robert said brusquely. Jane hated being called that, and felt the humiliation with especial keenness because she secretly agreed with him that her features were toad-like—the broad features, eyes slightly bugged, narrow hips and long skinny legs. That those eyes were an usually pretty hazel, that her breasts were beautifully shaped, that her face was almost pretty when she truly smiled, which was rare, were of no consequence to a woman used to focusing on her faults.

Miserably she stood and came toward her tormentor. Her eyes were wide with terror. "Stop looking like I'm going to kill you, girl. I just want to get to know you better. See what you're made of. I like to learn your strengths and weaknesses, as it were." Jane barely heard him, her heart thudding too loudly in her ears. She obeyed when he told her to raise her arms, and offered no protest as he Velcroed her wrists and ankles to the frame so that her body was open to him. He stretched her legs and arms just slightly past comfortable, leaving her completely vulnerable to his touch. He adjusted the frame so that her head was resting reasonably comfortably against the bars.

"Get ready now, you're going up," he said, though at first Jane didn't know what he meant. She found out as he tilted the frame back slightly, lifting Jane off her feet. This put her body at a 45-degree angle with the floor, so that her spread pussy was completely exposed to Robert's eye and hand. She gasped and struggled briefly, feeling a loss of balance and control as her feet left the ground. She felt she was going to fall, but in fact she was securely bound and totally at his mercy.

Robert tested her straps, making sure she was secure. Gently he leaned over her and kissed her mouth. Jane's eyes were squeezed shut, he observed, and this gave him an idea. Going to the toy chest he had carried in with him, he opened it and pulled out a long thick piece of black satin, which he tied around Jane's head, effectively blinding her. Some people got more frightened when you blindfolded them; they felt more out of control. Others were able to relax more, because they couldn't see what was happening, and were able to remove themselves from it; go with the flow more. He was curious to see which type Jane was. Not that it mattered. He would do what he liked no matter how she responded.

The first thing he did was take a tube of bright cherry red lipstick. Jane was trembling as she turned her head away. "Hold still, frog. I'm going to make you a little more attractive. You're pale as death. You really need to get out more." Unaware of the irony of his own statement, he took her chin in his hand, forcing her to turn back to him. Jane's head twitched and he ordered, "Hold still, stupid! You'll smear it!" Jane realized he was applying lipstick to her mouth. She felt the soft tip and smelled the particular scent of fine lipstick as he thickly applied it. She jerked when she felt the makeup being applied to one nipple and then the other.

He stood back to admire the garish red of her mouth in her pale thin face, and the lovely contrast to the black satin covering her eyes. The nipples, now blood-red against lovely white skin, made her look like a painted whore, and he liked the effect. "Very nice," he murmured, deciding she wasn't quite so ugly after all. Every woman had something appealing about her; you just had to bring it out.

"Are you scared?" he whispered close to her ear. Jane jumped. "You don't have to answer; your breathing gives you away. Slow it down, frog. You're going to be here a long time. Slow it down and just relax. You might even enjoy this. It's not all suffering and pain here at our house, slave girl. There is some pleasure, too. You would be wise to take it while you can, because my dear Brenda has very different ideas about how our toys are to be treated."

Jane shivered, believing him completely. She shuddered as he drew one finger down her side. And then his other hand was on her other side as he faced her, tracing sweeping circles across her body. She could feel his hot breath against her as he tickled and teased her flesh. It didn't hurt at least, thank God, she thought.

Gently he cupped first one breast, then the other, enjoying the slight solid heft of each one. They were firm and high and looked so pretty with the cherry red nipples. Slowly, he bent and licked the left one and then the right.

Though still deeply afraid, her body began responding to something which actually felt nice, if circumstances were different. Neither Tom nor Brian had ever put their mouths on her breasts, and she hadn't realized her nipples were so sensitive. Robert bit gently on one nubbin, and then on the other, pulling them out, making them harden. Jane moaned slightly and Robert grinned with pleasure at her response. The cunt liked it! She had potential, this little pussy. He would explore it fully.

"Does it feel good, frog? Answer me truthfully."

Feeling heat in her face, knowing she was blushing, Jane nodded and stammered, "Yes, sir."

"Sir?" Robert was amused. "Ah, Brenda's been schooling you in the art of proper address, huh? She's our formal one, *Mistress Brenda*," he said, derisively. Then he remembered she was probably watching and listening over the video camera so he said a little louder, "She has a better sense of that sort of thing. So, yes, call me 'sir', pussy girl."

"Now, as I said, it's not *all* pain. But you can't fully appreciate pleasure unless you throw in a little pain, that's what I say." He slapped her face, suddenly. Jane, who couldn't see what was coming, cried out in shock and pain. Then his mouth was on hers, smearing her lipstick onto his own lips, not so much kissing her as raping her mouth with his tongue. His fingers found and twisted her nipples. She gasped against his mouth, which was still pressed against hers, as he bit and sucked her lips and pressed past her teeth with his tongue.

He pulled away, watching the girl, still gasping as she tried to catch her breath. She looked like such a tart, with her lipstick smeared on her mouth, and those bright red nipples erect and distended from his not so kind attentions. He loved the confusion he could render, mixing the pleasure and pain, reducing his subject to raw lust, and raw terror, a most potent combination in his twisted mind.

Robert trailed his hand down her belly to her curly pubic hair and just below to her spread open cunt. He massaged the folds, his face bent near her, his touch light as air. "You still smell like piss, dirty frog. You really should bathe more often." Jane flinched, again feeling the dull heat of humiliation at his degrading words. She longed to close her legs, but she couldn't move at all.

"You know, Brenda would smack this nasty cunt for stinking, just like *this*," Robert slapped her pussy suddenly, causing Jane to scream, though she couldn't move away. "But I forgive you, frog, since I know you're kind of tied up right now," he laughed. "Ah, poor baby, I smacked your little pussy too hard, didn't I? It's all red, let me smooth away the pain," he said, his voice gentle now. Slowly, with fingers light as feathers, he spread her folds, revealing the little hooded clit. Gently he touched it, and then moved away, lightly massaging and teasing her pussy. He lowered himself so that he could tongue her cunt, not really caring if it tasted a little like piss. That was just an act he put on to further degrade her.

She jumped when she felt the warm tongue against her flesh, not knowing at first what it was. When she realized, she was mortified, and tried in vain to shut her legs. She secretly believed her private parts were dirty, no matter how often she showered, and was horrified that he was putting his mouth *down there!* But again, she was restrained, and had no choice but to submit to his attentions. Robert licked carefully, slowly, circling round her clit but never quite touching it. Without her even being aware what he was doing, he was training her body to desire the kisses. After several minutes he licked directly on the little clit, making Jane squirm and sigh slightly. At once he pulled away, aware of the desire he was building up in her.

Again and again he teased and suckled her, going just near, but not close enough, to the center of her desire. After a good twenty minutes of teasing, he stayed right at her clit, licking rough and fast, pulling a deep guttural moan from his captive, making her arch up into his mouth. He felt her body begin to shudder with impending orgasm and again pulled his mouth away. She slumped back, her breathing labored and though she didn't speak, he could tell she was frustrated and beyond embarrassment at this point. She wanted to come, the little slut.

He laughed softly and began the sexual torture again. She was so sensitized to his touch that she again began to come as he neared her clit, and again he pulled away. Over and over he teased her until at last he didn't stop, and she began to shudder and whine, a high pitched keening that startled both him and herself as she came for the first time in her life at the hands of another.

Robert sat back, quite satisfied with her performance, though of course he didn't say so. He watched her breasts heave prettily as she slowly regained her composure, as much as she could, being tied spread eagle and tilted off the ground. Her body was bathed in a sheen of sweat and was flushed pink from exertion and orgasm. As her breathing slowly returned to normal he said, "Now, that was a gift, and you'll have to give me one in return. Have you ever sucked cock?"

She shook her head, her expression one of ill-disguised disgust. "No, I didn't think so. Dried up little prune, weren't you, back in your past life. Huh, frog? You just need a man to give you a good fucking and show you what's what, but you didn't find one, did you? No, I can just see you, hunched over your frozen dinner, watching *Lifetime* on T.V., reading your boring little novels and going to sleep, night after night, never even dreaming there was a prince charming out there to kiss the frog and set her free." In fact, he was very near the mark, which made his comments cut that much more.

"Well, don't worry anymore, sweetheart, because Robert's here to teach you to be a proper slut. You are going to learn to suck cock like a pro, free of charge. Now, for starters, I'm going to fit this little gag into your mouth, to teach you how to relax your throat." As Robert spoke, he untied the blindfold, leaving Jane to squint in the bright light of the room. As her eyes adjusted, she focused on what he was holding. It was a gag, the center of which was composed of a hard plastic phallus shaped like a small penis. Mercifully, it was relatively small, only four inches or so long and not too thick. "A beginner model," Robert said, grinning, reading her mind. "Open wide."

He pressed the cold plastic against her lips and poor Jane had no choice but to comply. Slipping the gag in place, he secured it behind her head. "Don't you look pretty," he smiled, watching her eyes tear as she tried to adjust to the offending object pressed against her soft palate.

"Just for good measure," he added, grinning evilly, "let's not leave your cunt out of the fun." So saying, Robert took a dildo which was much larger than the penis gag, and slipped it into a harness before rudely shoving it up her snatch. Jane emitted a grunt of pain from behind the plastic cock in her mouth. Robert said, "Lucky for you that you were still wet from your orgasm, slut. It would have hurt way worse otherwise!" He buckled the harness around her slim waist so that the dildo would stay buried deep in her pussy. As a final touch, he replaced the satin blindfold. There he left her, bound, blinded, gagged, and stuffed, to muse on her fate.

The minutes ticked slowly by. Though she was bound and immobilized, her mind was churning with what had just happened to her. Confusion was paramount, as she tried unsuccessfully to grapple with the outrage at having been abused and tortured, and the secret pleasure of the wild orgasm that had been wrenched from her without her consent or even understanding. She could still hear her own piercing scream as she came echoing in her mind.

And not only had he forced her body to react in that sexual way, but his horrid wife had probably been watching on the closed-circuit camera, getting off on Jane's humiliation and total loss of control. She flushed here, alone, just thinking about it all. And yet. And yet she couldn't deny that instance when pain was obliterated and pleasure rode roughshod over everything else, shutting down her mind, her fears, her consciousness as it swept her body into a moment of pure delight. Remembering it now, she felt her vaginal muscles contract slightly against the invading dildo rammed up her cunt.

She heard something and stiffened, her musings forgotten. Unable to scream, to talk, to see, to move, Jane's hearing had become especially acute. She felt she could almost hear the tumblers of the lock falling into place as the key scraped in its hole. She heard the door open and the sharp click of high heels against the floor. She heard who must be Brenda come close to her and circle her slowly. Not a word was said and Jane began to tremble with fear and anticipation, the silence weighing on her like a stone.

It was broken with a swishing sound and a loud crack as a flogger struck Jane's ass without warning. Jane's scream was muffled by the penis gag as she jerked away from the whip. "I want you to count, frog," commanded Brenda, who was dressed today in what Robert called her Mistress Outfit. She was wearing a tightly cut leather bodice that pushed her large breasts together, creating a deep cleavage. Her miniskirt molded flatteringly against her curvaceous form, and garters peeked out from its hem, holding up sheer black stockings that hugged her long, shapely legs. Black patent leather six-inch heels completed the outfit.

At close to six feet, with large breasts and broad hips, Brenda was an imposing figure. Her long, dark, red hair hung loose over the black leather vest. In her mid-thirties, she was still beautiful, and today her green eyes sparkled as she wielded her favorite flogger. She did love to give a good whipping, and this slut had definitely earned hers.

Brenda had watched and listened to Robert's introduction to the sensual pleasures via the closed-circuit camera, as Robert had guessed she would. Her own hand had crept to her pussy as she watched her husband expertly bring that slave cunt to orgasm. She knew precisely what Jane was feeling. Robert could always drive a woman wild. His tongue was like a magic wand, drawing the passion out of you no matter how you resisted. Watching him lick and fondle their new toy was both exciting and enraging. If she had probed her own feelings, Brenda would have had to admit that the jealousy was as much a factor in her arousal as the voyeuristic pleasure she took in watching her man use another.

Then she would feel her blood heat with passion and with that familiar jealous rage which lent such fire to the beatings her slaves got after Robert used them. Today was no exception. "I want you to count each lash, and then you will thank me that many times for your whipping. Am I understood?" she punctuated the question with the second strike, this time to Jane's back.

Jane jerked in pain and surprise, but managed to nod her understanding. She wished she could faint like the first day, but she remained mercilessly alert and aware. Now only muffled groans, whimpers, and the whoosh and smack of the whip could be heard as she received each lash. Jane could never anticipate where the next blow would land. It might be her back, ass, or thigh. Brenda would move from spot to spot, and then hit one tender area repeatedly until Jane would actually feel relief to be struck at another, less tender spot.

When at last the whipping stopped, Jane's skin was on fire and her face was flushed with exertion. Brenda removed the gag, though she didn't untie the hapless woman. The thick red lipstick had smeared over Jane's mouth and chin, making her look like a little girl who had gotten into red icing. Brenda snorted derisively, saying, "Your face is a mess, lipstick all over you like some back-street whore."

Brenda shifted the frame so that Jane was standing upright, though the dildo was still firmly embedded in her cunt. She pulled off the blindfold to reveals eyes wet with tears. Jane opened and closed her jaw several times, relieved to have the offending object removed at last. Brenda stood in front of her, regal in her outfit, eyes flashing, breasts heaving from having beaten the poor woman still bound in front of her.

"Well," she said, waiting. "One thank-you for each lash. Get it wrong and we start again."

"T-thank you, Mistress," began Jane, trying not to cry.

"That's one. Go on, girl. Are you a total idiot? Can't you count? Or do you want the whip again?" She raised her arm menacingly, whistling the whip in the air next to Jane, who flinched.

"Thank you, thank you, thank you, thank you," Jane hurried to interject. She counted off twenty-five thank-you's, praying she had got it right, terrified of another whipping on her tender aching flesh.

Grudgingly Brenda said, "All right. So you can count. Later I'll require that you beg me to know what you can do to *show* your thanks for getting the beating you deserve. And you do deserve it, don't you, whore, for leading my husband on like that?"

Jane didn't know at first what she meant, and then slowly a glimmer of understanding pierced her, as she realized Brenda might actually be jealous of her husband's "attentions." The thought dumbfounded her for a moment. How could this tall, voluptuous woman with that wild mane of dark red hair possibly be jealous of a short, skinny little person with thin hair and no curves to speak of? It was crazy! And to say that Jane was leading him on, when she had been bound and forced, was beyond absurd. But then, this whole nightmare made no sense.

Seeing Brenda's dark flashing eyes and the hard line of her mouth, Jane knew she was in a no-win situation. She was damned no matter what, to suffer at Brenda's hand, to suffer at Robert's hand. All she could do was try to find ways to minimize it, and to stay alive. Escape at this point seemed impossible.

Escape. She realized as the thought popped into her head that while it was impossible now, maybe it wouldn't always be! If she could learn the crazy game they were playing, try to figure out the rules, maybe she could somehow get herself out of this horrible plight. They were both crazy, that was clear, but maybe somewhere there were chinks, ways to gain more freedom, to gain their trust, to get out of this room! To save herself.

No. She wouldn't think on that now. One step at a time. The most important thing now was to learn the rules. She was already coming to realize that Brenda was the formidable one. Brenda was the one with whom she really had to deal. Because while Robert saw her strictly as an object to be used and debased, Brenda understood and appreciated that she was human, with all the frailties that implied. Brenda would be the one to overcome.

Chapter 3

VIGNETTES IN PLEASURE AND THE PAIN

Jane was bound to the gynecological table set in the center of her little prison, pelvis slightly raised by a pillow thrust under her hips. She was positioned so that her head was hanging off the front of the table. Brenda waved the glittering silver speculum at her, and then smeared it with lubricant before inserting it into Jane's spread vagina. She spread the phalanges until Jane screamed from the pressure. Brenda hissed, "Shut up, cunt. I'm stretching you so Robert can fuck you properly. You haven't even seen his cock yet, have you?"

As if on cue, Robert entered the room, wrapped only in a small towel around his loins. A thick gold chain lay glittering against his massive hairy chest. He let the towel drop and strode over to Jane's head, which was positioned so he could drive his cock down her throat. First he moved into her line of vision so she could see the huge penis of which he was so proud and which Brenda also prized. Jane almost fainted from the sight of it. Poor Brian had not been well endowed, though Jane didn't know this until now. The thought of that thing entering her caused her vaginal walls to clench involuntarily against the cold hard steel shoved deep inside of her. But Robert wasn't planning on fucking her yet. No. First she was going to learn the art of cock sucking. Trial by fire, since her only experience so far was the little plastic phallus they had locked in place as a gag. Now he crouched over her, so that the tip of his cock touched her lips.

"Open your mouth, bitch," Brenda growled. "Don't you dare deny my husband!" She opened the speculum wider as she spoke, and Jane cried out. Very reluctantly she opened her mouth, and Robert eased his cock into it. It felt hot and smooth and she could smell the musky odor of his arousal. He allowed her a few minutes to get used to the invading presence and then, without warning, he glided his erection into her throat. As he drove his cock down, her gag reflex tightened around it and she began to choke. He held it there, catching Brenda's eye as they watched her writhe on the table, feeling her panic as he blocked her windpipe.

He pulled back slowly, and she gasped for breath. Again he entered, slow and smooth, forcing her to take it again, choke-fucking her with his cock. Again and again he gagged her, released her, and gagged her again, until at last, spent, she relaxed against the invasion. He continued to thrust in and out of her mouth, deep-throating her until he came, pulling out in time to cover her face and tits with his seed.

Brenda withdrew the speculum, leaving Jane's pussy gaping. She took a whip and shoved the handle into Jane's cunt. "Don't you dare let it fall out. Keep it in place or I'll whip you with it!" Brenda ordered the slave.

Turning to her husband, she observed that he was holding his penis, still semi-erect. "Gotta pee," he informed her, moving toward the door.

"So? Do it here? We have the perfect toilet right here. She's not going anywhere." Robert looked at his wife, a slow smile creeping across his face.

"Go ahead," Brenda coaxed him. "You know she deserves it.

Hell, she's lucky to get your piss. She's lucky to get anything you offer her."

Robert nodded, stroking his penis as he stood over the poor girl. "Golden shower time, slut." Jane squeezed her eyes shut as the warm piss splashed on her belly, her breasts, her pussy, and her face. Robert waved his cock lewdly from side to side, covering the poor miserable woman in his urine, marking her like some wild animal.

Though she was desperately hoping they would release her, the couple let her alone, tied to the table, her arms bound tightly at her sides. With sticky cum on her face and tits, a whip handle sticking lewdly out of her cunt, and dripping with piss, the bound and spread woman was thoroughly frightened and humiliated. She knew that she had to keep the whip handle in place or get the promised beating. It was too much. She was spent; exhausted by the ordeal. Closing her eyes, she felt herself slipping mercifully away.

Robert came to her later, unlocking her from her shackles. He pulled out the whip handle, which had remained embedded inside of her. He ordered her to stand, but saw that she was unable to do so without his assistance. Weakly she stood, swaying slightly, trying to cover herself with her arms. Robert quickly hosed her down and she was actually grateful for the cold spray that washed away the sticky cum and nasty piss.

Still shivering and naked, she was ordered to lie on the floor and spread her legs. Robert then secured each ankle and wrist to the eyehooks set at strategic intervals. "I'm not done washing you yet. Your little cunt is still very dirty. Dirty, nasty little cunt," he murmured, as he adjusted the nozzle of the hose to a more directed spray.

As he aimed the cold spray of water at her sex, Jane's pelvis jerked, but she couldn't get away. The spray was intense, stimulating her sensitive labia and clitoris. She was unable to close her legs. A pressure that wasn't entirely unpleasant began to build in her loins. She felt a heat that mixed strangely with the cold of the water spray. He held the spray against her, not caring that he was getting thoroughly wet himself, as he watched her arch against the onslaught of water.

Even chained as she was, she was aware of the sexual tension building in her, and against which she was powerless to resist. Actually it felt good, one of the few pleasant sensations she had had since being abducted. Robert held the spray steady now, a pounding stream against her sensitive center.

"Oh, God," the words were wrenched from her as the water forced the unwilling woman to orgasm. Still, Robert aimed the water stream at her as she vainly arched and bucked in her chains. Pleasure began to melt into irritation as sensation moved from arousal to nausea.

Jane began to beg, "Please! I can't! Please, stop, no more . . ." Robert laughed, knowing precisely that he was taking her from pleasure to pain, all wrought by his hand, under his control.

Finally, he turned off the hose. Jane's body, which was an arc of protest, collapsed against the hard floor, splashing in the puddle of water beneath her. "I own you," Robert whispered, as he turned the water away from the drenched and exhausted woman. "Don't forget it."

As he left her there, wet and bound, he didn't hear her whisper, "No. You don't."

He returned sometime later, ready to play with his toy some more. He untied her and allowed her to dry herself. He allowed her eat an apple and drink some water. He even tidied her room, wiping down the floor with some towels while she rested in a corner, eyeing him carefully, trying to make the apple last.

Then he said, "Time for lesson number two. First, take off my shorts. Do it sexy, like you want to do it. You know you do anyway. No woman can resist my huge cock." Jane would have given anything to be able to resist it, but she complied with his orders. "This time you get to seduce me. You're not tied down. You get a chance to show me what a lover you can be. You can use your hands. Be gentle. Don't go too fast. Take your time. Pretend it's a delicious lollipop. If you do it good, I'll bring you a nice treat." Food is a strong motivator when you're hungry. The apple had only barely satisfied her most immediate need for sustenance. She was ravenous.

Screwing her eyes shut, Jane allowed his erect cock to enter her mouth. She tried to obey his running litany of commands. When she hesitated, he took his cock and slapped her cheeks with it. As he slapped her he ordered, "I want you to take it in slowly. Like it's a delicate and delicious candy." Reluctantly, Jane opened her mouth and Robert slid his cock in. "Yeah. That's it, baby. No! Slow down." He slapped her face with his hard cock.

Nudging it back into her mouth he ordered, "Lick it up and down before you take it in your throat." Jane tried desperately to obey. She must have pleased him because he moaned, "Yeah, oh, yeah. Now, ring the head with your tongue. Ah, yeah." She closed her lips and began to move up and down, creating a little suction with her mouth. "Open wide, cunt. I'm gonna fuck your face." Finesse was forgotten as he rammed his erection down Jane's throat, making her lose her balance as she knelt before him. Grabbing her hair, he held her in place, pushing his cock in and out of her mouth, using her like the fuck toy he saw her as.

He didn't care that he was gagging her repeatedly with his huge cock. In fact, it turned him on. By the time he came, Jane's jaw was aching, tears were streaming down her cheeks, and her knees were bruised and stiff on the hard wooden floor. When his hot salty semen shot down her throat, she had no choice but to swallow it.

When at last he left, she waited impatiently, hoping he would return with the food he had promised. Instead he returned with Brenda. Poor Jane was again ordered to kneel in front of Robert, while Brenda sat off to the side, watching the show.

"Get me hard again, you ugly frog," Robert commanded, "and show me that you *like* it." Brenda smiled, pleased with his choice of adjective, as he had known she would be. Hiding her reluctance, and still clinging to the hope of food, Jane tried to show enthusiasm and excite Robert, while at the same time trying to balance that enthusiasm with care, knowing that jealous Brenda was closely observing her. Jane was more awkward under Brenda's relentless eye, and Robert slapped her repeatedly with his wet cock, humiliating her completely.

Pretending to lose patience, Robert grabbed Jane's head in his large hands. Holding her still and rutting into her face, at last Robert came a third time that day down her raw throat. He pushed her back, causing her to fall back onto the floor. "About time, cunt," he said, as if displeased. In fact, she really had outdone herself this time, slowly licking and caressing him with her tongue and then opening her throat to his invasion with an almost practiced ease. Still, he wouldn't let Brenda see the pleasure he took from her. Instead, he grinned meanly as she sprawled naked at his feet. "We'll bring you something to eat, since a promise is a promise, little frog."

They left together and Jane lay where she had fallen, tears slipping silently from her eyes. A few minutes later Robert did in fact return, with two bananas, a can of cold Coke, and an entire bag of Oreos. Jane lay very still where she had dropped, hoping he would leave her there. He did. Brenda was calling him and, after three orgasms, he'd had enough of the frog for the night.

Jane ate both bananas and half of the cookies. Her stomach hurt but she didn't care. At least she wasn't hungry! She hid the other cookies around the room, hoping she wasn't being observed. She also hid the Coke. Her water bottle would suffice for now, though the water that came from it tasted of the plastic it was made of. She had already become adept at sucking on the little metal tube in her cage. She may be treated like an animal, but, she reminded herself, she was still alive. And because they had left where she had fallen, they hadn't put her into the cage, and they hadn't locked the cage door with her inside. Life, even life here, had its bright points. She had food in her belly and an entire night of freedom in her little prison. She was almost happy.

The problem with getting the food was that her body was eventually forced to expel the waste. She was used to peeing in the little drain now, and barely thought about it as she squatted over it and did her business as efficiently as possible, using a little strip of paper from the neat pile she had prepared. But now Jane had to move her bowels. For the first week she had been too terrified and had so little to eat that she hadn't had to face this issue. Constipation born of clenched bowels and little food had so far spared Jane the embarrassment of being forced to defecate on newspaper on the floor. Now she felt the push of need as her intestines protested for release. She had held it in as long as she could and now knew she would have to use the dreaded newspaper and relieve herself. The thought of her shit sitting there for her jailers to see was almost more humiliating than she could bear.

It was early morning, just after dawn, if she could judge by the pale light glimmering in through her little window. At least it was unlikely that either of them was up and watching her on the closed-circuit T.V. Going over to the newspapers, she squatted tentatively and tried to move her bowels, keeping her legs spread like she was at a camp ground behind a bush. She managed to relieve herself, and was forced to use the strips of newspaper as her toilet paper. She tried to clean herself as best she could. The spigot was off limits without their presence and she didn't dare to use it.

There was nowhere to dispose of the waste. Jane rolled the newspaper up tightly, and used more papers from the stack in the corner to further bundle it. She put the package in the corner and tried to forget about it. When Brenda came in later that morning she held her nose and said, "Frog, you disgusting little animal! It smells like a pig farm in here!" Jane bowed her head, deeply ashamed, but also enraged that she had been put into this situation. Of course they knew she had no choice, and yet they would tease and humiliate her for doing what her body required. Brenda made an elaborate show of removing the offensive little package, dropping it into a large trash bag she brought in for the purpose.

Then Brenda did something Jane didn't know could be done. Using a little stepladder, Brenda climbed up to the window. She fished out her key ring and inserted a little key into a small round lock under the panel, set in the molding. As she slid the window silently up she said, "Let's get a little air in here, frog."

Jane, who had retreated to her cage, turned away, hoping against hope that Brenda would leave, and leave the window open! She sensed instinctively that if she seemed to take notice of the lovely fresh air floating into the room that Brenda would take it away by shutting the window. Jane's heart was pounding at the revelation before her, as she tried to appear unaware. As if the gods were intervening on her behalf, Robert called to Brenda at just that moment, and Brenda said, "I'll be right back; don't go anywhere." Laughing at her own little joke, she left the room, locking it behind her. Jane waited a few moments to make sure her jailer wasn't coming back right away, and then slowly she walked over to the window.

She stood on tiptoe, trying to get a breath of the fresh air wafting in. It smelled so sweet! Like clover and honey and fresh rain. When she had been free she had rarely noticed the weather, except when it inconvenienced her by raining. Now she felt a longing that was physical in its intensity. To leave this little room which had become her shrunken universe. To be free! This window could open! It was a small window, but she was a small person, made smaller still by her enforced diet. At 5'3" and barely 100 pounds, she could possibly wriggle her way through. If she could get up that high.

How had she missed that little lock before? She examined it now, seeing that it was cut neatly into the molding, very hard to see unless you knew to look for it. She must get that key. Somehow, she must get that key. Somehow, she *would* get that key.

Robert liked to watch women take a shit. There was something so degrading, so wildly sexy about their total debasement as he spied on this most private and intimate of acts. Unfortunately, though he had spent many hours secretly watching Jane on the closed-circuit T.V., she hadn't moved her bowels in front of him. Then, when she finally did it, as reported by Brenda, she had waited until they were sleeping, the little sneak! Well, today that would change.

This particular afternoon Brenda was busy getting beautiful at the hair salon. To make sure he got what he was after, Robert decided to give the frog a special treat. A lovely bowl of chocolate ice cream. But the syrup he squirted over it was laced with maltitol, a sweetener with a decided laxative effect. He watched her eat it, though he could see she would rather have been left alone. He would make sure she ate every bite.

Several hours later, he was pleased to observe through the camera that Jane was clasping her belly in seeming distress. Yes, she should be heading to the newspaper soon.

He wasn't disappointed. Slowly Jane rose from her blankets and moved to the paper, still clutching her belly. She squatted and Robert watched with eager anticipation, leaning forward toward the screen. He massaged his cock at the kitchen table, his hand flying over the rigid member as he watched the little slut relieve herself on the papers, just like a dog. Even though she was alone, he saw the dark blush of shame spread along her cheeks. The maltitol had done its work, leaving her stool a runny gooey mess. She tried to clean herself at the spigot, an act strictly forbidden and which he duly noted. At last, she carefully rolled the soiled newspaper and set it against the wall.

To his added delight, she squatted over the drain and peed. Robert spurted then and there on the table, jerking forward as he came hard. Just then he heard the sound of the electric garage door opening. Brenda was back. Quickly he tucked his spent cock back into his pants. Robert was sprawled on the living room couch, and appeared to be engrossed in a novel, sipping a soda, when Brenda entered, her auburn hair highlighted with blonde and her long red nails freshly lacquered.

Though Robert omitted his use of maltitol (Brenda found his obsession with feces peculiar), he didn't omit the fact that he had seen Jane taking a dump and then using the spigot without permission. Brenda was eager to make the little bitch pay for that one, as he had known she would be. She seemed to take special pleasure in humiliating the wretched girl.

Brenda changed into play clothes and then they burst into her room, chiding Jane for the smell; shaming her for an act she couldn't control. When Brenda casually informed her that using the spigot without permission was forbidden and that she would be punished, Jane flushed a deep pink, feeling the heat of her shame prickle in her scalp. If they had seen that, they had witnessed what went before it!

"Time for a spanking for that one!" Brenda announced. She was dressed in her favorite red leather, this time skintight leggings that made her look as if her legs had been dipped in shiny red paint. She sported a matching vest that barely concealed her ample bosom. Robert was in jeans, his massive chest bare as usual.

A spanking. Jane's dad had spanked her until she was well into her teens. He let her keep her panties on, but he would use his hand, cupping the palm to make it sting. That didn't happen often though; Jane usually was able to stay out of trouble. She was an expert at melting into the background. But here there was no getting away.

Still, she could take a spanking, she figured. How bad could it be, compared to whips and crops? She was to find out. First they bound her wrists to chains dangling from the ceiling. Then Robert adjusted the pulley mechanism until Jane was actually lifted from the floor, her full weight suspended by her wrists.

They took turns, using their open palms to smack her small bottom. Each smack resounded with an echo in the empty room, followed by her cries.

When she began to beg for them to let her down, they gagged her, using the red ball gag so that her tongue was thrust back, rendering her mute. Her thin body swayed with each blow, with each hand that left its angry print on her ass and thighs. When at last they stopped, Brenda leaned over and said in a low voice, "Next time obey the rules, cunt. This is what happens to bad little girls who don't listen to their betters."

Jane was strapped over a low stool, ass up, head down. Brenda took a small butt plug and greased it with lubricant. "This plug is just the little starter version," she obligingly explained. "Stretch you out a little. Robert was rather brutal with his cock that first day. Trial by fire, he likes to say." As Brenda prattled on, she inserted the little plug into poor Jane's ass. It didn't hurt until the last bit, which was flared, slipped past her unwilling sphincter. Jane grunted in pain.

"Hurts? Oh, well. You'll get used to it. Robert does like to fuck women in the ass. I won't let him *near* my ass, so he has to use you little slave girls." Even in her discomfort and embarrassment at being tied down and reamed like this, Jane had the wherewithal to wonder who the other little slave girls were. Were they still here? Secured in other little prisons scattered throughout the house? Or were they gone, murdered after being sexually tortured for days, weeks, months? She shivered at the thought.

Brenda withdrew the plug with a sudden jerk, but the relief was momentary, as she was preparing a larger, thicker plug for another invasion. "Oh, God, please!" Jane cried out as Brenda pressed this one mercilessly home. She was breathing hard, and all her muscles were clenched, making the presence of the plug that much harder to take. Her wrists were loosely tied in front of her, her thighs strapped with leather belts to the low stool, knees resting on the floor.

"You look like such a slut pig, frog. I'm gonna leave you for a while like that. Get you good and ready for Robert. You really should thank me for this; I'm getting you nice and stretched so you won't bleed like that first time. A little advice, sugar. Relax. You're so rigid you're gonna break that thing off!" Brenda bent down and patted Jane's bottom, giving the plug a little tap, pressing it in just a little further. Then she left the room, not even bothering to lock it; Jane wasn't going anywhere right now.

Jane realized, despite the flippant manner in which it had been offered, that Brenda's advice was sound. She needed to relax her body. Even her jaw was clenched so tightly she could feel the dull throb of pain in her temples. With a conscious effort, she began to relax her muscles, starting with her jaw and tongue, moving slowly down her body until she got to her poor ass. Slowly her body adjusted to the fat phallus lodged inside of her.

When Robert came in about twenty minutes later, Jane's breathing had slowed and she was not exactly resting comfortably, but at least she wasn't in panic mode. Robert was wearing a jock strap and nothing else. His burly, heavily muscled frame came into view in front of Jane, as thickly muscled thighs matted with dark hair came into her line of vision.

"Bren's got you all ready for me, eh? Well, I hope she didn't open you up too much! I like 'em tight! Nice tight little virgin assholes for me to fuck. That's what I like. Right, Bren?" Jane realized then that Brenda was in the room. Somehow that made it much worse. She knew she was going to be anally raped again, but having Brenda there as a witness made it that much more shameful and harder to bear for poor Jane.

"Don't worry, Robbie. One little butt plug for half an hour isn't going to ruin your little virgin asshole here. Let's pull it out and see." She withdrew the plug, eliciting a grunt from Jane. How she longed to close her legs. She could only imagine the picture she must present now, bound with her ass raised in the air, asshole still stretched from the offending plug. Flames of heat moved through her chest and face. But they weren't looking at her face.

"Suck me, baby," Robert said to his wife, who knelt in front of him, eagerly pulling his cock from its jock strap. Brenda was dressed only in yellow silk panties and a matching bra. She wore several bejeweled bracelets that clanked as she moved her hands slowly up and down Robert's shaft, and gently cupped his heavy, hairy balls. Long golden earrings glittered through her auburn hair. She took his penis expertly back deep into her throat. "Oh, yeah," Robert moaned, letting his head fall back and closing his eyes. "No one can do that like you can, baby." Brenda smiled behind the big erection stuffed in her mouth. She was smugly certain that he was right; no one could give head like she could. No matter how many lessons the bastard gave to these slave girls. Now she put all of her subtle skill into arousing him to his hardest possible. Even though it sometimes made her a teeny bit jealous, Brenda did like to watch the show when he fucked these virgin girls.

"You're ready, baby," she murmured, "Oh boy are you ready." She stood, wiping her mouth with the back of one hand. Let's see what you can do now to this little whore. Don't be too gentle, either. She can take it." Robert eagerly positioned himself behind the hapless girl, his penis bobbing at her still gaping asshole. He pressed it slowly at first, just lodging the thick head into her. Then he thrust himself into her in one hard motion. Jane's muscles contracted against his penis, and any thoughts of relaxation were obliterated as panic rose like a gorge inside of her. The ironic result of her body's resistance was extra pleasure for Robert, as her muscles clenched and milked his rock hard cock.

Brenda had moved in front of Jane. She sat cross-legged on the floor in front of the poor woman and smoothed her tangled blonde hair from her brow. Jane was sweating, and her eyes were clenched shut. Her mouth was open in a little "o" of pain. Brenda felt a lovely pull in her loins. There was nothing as erotic to her as watching her charges suffer at her and her husband's hands. She loved to see them, naked, bound, contorting, and writhing in helpless pain and terror. She slipped a hand into her silk panties and felt her own sweet wetness. She should make this bitch lick her, while she was being butt fucked. But that would be too much work right now. Jane was such a frigid little bitch and she'd have to forcibly direct her every move. No, for right now she'd do herself. Just sit back and watch the fun.

Robert was in a rhythm now, thrusting hard and then pulling back slowly. He would pause a moment or two and then *thrust*, hard, into Jane's tortured asshole. His head was back, the veins distended in his thick neck. The skinny little woman tied down beneath him looked like a rag doll as he held her still with his strong hands spread on her hips.

"Does it hurt, Janie?" Brenda leaned down, whispering to the girl. Jane nodding, eyes still squeezed shut, wondering if Brenda would somehow take pity, though knowing at the same time that of course she would not.

"Good," Brenda responded, an evil grin on her face. She began to rub her pussy, pulling the silk aside. Robert looked down, seeing his wife with her hand buried in her panties, the dark auburn pubic hair peeking through the fabric. He thrust harder, making Jane scream. As he picked up his tempo, Brenda picked up hers. They were both using Jane to make themselves come. She truly was no more than an object for them to debase. Brenda came first, panting and undulating on the floor, licking her lips and flashing her green eyes at Robert. Jane witnessed none of this; her eyes squeezed shut in pain and self-protection.

Brenda's attempt at a sensual display was mostly wasted on Robert, whose eyes were closed now as he rutted into Jane, slamming himself against her, balls slapping her small bottom. He grunted low and gutturally, shooting his seed into her and then holding her still, forcing her to bear his considerable weight for a moment or two before rolling off of her, his cock slipping out of her with a little pop.

Jane was whimpering quietly when the two of them noticed her again. Brenda wanted to leave her bound, but Robert convinced her it would be better to release her so she could clean up herself and save them the trouble later. "You can use the spigot, frog. Clean yourself up; you're a mess." They left the room together and Jane slowly rolled off the low stool. She lay still for several moments, and then gingerly touched her bottom. It was wet with semen and bits of feces, her own. Thoroughly horrified by this discovery, her humiliation hardened into a rage that these fiends could do something like this!

Slowly she crawled to the spigot and turned on the water. It was cold but it would clean off her own filth and his nasty gooey deposit. At least there was no blood this time. It had been painful, but not as bad as a caning. And it was over. They were gone, for now.

Chapter 4

DEGRADATION

Brenda liked the verbal humiliation almost as much as the physical. She loved to tie them up and whip them, yes. She loved to watch Robert defile them with his cock and cum all over them. But she also loved to control them; to make them behave like the slaves they were, and all because she ordered them to. She loved power. Today she had Jane on the floor, kneeling with her hands behind her head.

"What are you, Jane?" she asked, her voice nonchalant, belying the iron will beneath it. She had just spent the last half hour training Jane in the expected responses and now Jane would be tested.

Jane mumbled something and Brenda said sharply, "Speak up, frog. I can't hear you!"

Louder this time, with eyes shifting away, Jane said, "I am a worthless cunt, Mistress."

"That's right," Brenda nodded, smiling slightly. "And what else are you?"

"A piece of ass made for your pleasure and my pain."

"Very good," Brenda liked that one. "And what else."

Jane paused. She was trying to remember, and then she did

remember, but didn't want to say it aloud. How she hated this woman. Brenda moved toward her menacingly and Jane sputtered, "A piece of shit. A nasty piece of shit." She bit her lips, bitterly ashamed and angry.

"That's right. A piece of shit not worth being on the bottom of my shoe. And yet we put up with you. At least for now. And you owe us thanks, because you know we could have killed you, but instead we keep you around, feeding you, housing you. You're lucky you're alive, you know that, don't you?"

Jane closed her eyes. She wanted to drop her arms, which were so tired, as she held them up behind her head, fingers locked to keep them from falling. She wanted to crawl back to her little cage and curl up, losing herself in sleep. Lately, she no longer thought in broader terms about escape. Just to get through this little ordeal and be left alone. Her time was measured by surviving each dreadful test they set for her, and being left alone for an hour, a day, a night.

She almost agreed now with Brenda; she was a worthless piece of shit. She had given up hope of ever being freed. She belonged to these people; they were her world. They controlled her every move. They decided when she ate, when she would be beaten, when she slept, if she lived or died.

She didn't know if anyone in the outside world even knew she was gone. They had certainly replaced her at work. She often went months without contacting anyone in her family so they probably didn't even know she was missing. The landlord would figure it out when he didn't get his rent. And maybe the police had traced her car. For all the good it did her. They would never find her. Who would ever think to look here?

No doubt Robert and Brenda were pillars of their community. Money bought you respectability. If she ever did get away, who would believe her story against theirs? She had never felt worthwhile, even before the abduction. And now this tall, statuesque woman standing imperiously before her, drilling it into her, "You are scum; you are a cunt; you are a whore; you deserve all that you get." Maybe she was right.

Anger was replaced with resignation as a tear slipped down Jane's cheek. Brenda, like any skilled predator, knew when the prey was weakening. Her voice now deceptively gentle, she moved in for the kill. "You are my little cunt, aren't you, Jane? My ugly, skinny, little slave. But don't you worry, sugar. Brenda will make it all better. Brenda will keep you safe. I won't let nasty Robert fuck your ass anymore, I promise. I'll feed you and take care of you. All you have to do right now is tell me again what a nasty little bitch you are, and that you deserve everything you get. And then I want you to crawl over here and kiss my feet. That's all you have to do. Then you can go to sleep. And when you wake up, there'll be a nice lunch for you."

Actually grateful for the kind tone in Brenda's words, actually grateful that she was going to be allowed to sleep after she did those few simple things, Jane dutifully parroted, "I'm your little cunt. Your ugly, little slave. I'm a nasty little bitch and I deserve whatever I get." She looked over toward Brenda to see if she approved. Brenda nodded regally and Jane slipped gratefully down, crawling over to lick Brenda's bare toes, her spirit subjugated, all anger seeped away, replaced by an awful resignation that was much more dangerous.

Robert had made much of his promises to fuck their frog, and Jane knew it would be soon. She found herself almost wanting it; at least it wasn't a beating. And it would certainly be better than the constant anal penetration he forced upon her.

Sex had been all right with Brian, though of course she knew there was no comparison—Brian had asked her permission; Robert would take what he regarded as his. His property, his toy, his piece of ass, his *frog*.

As Jane lay in her cage, she thought about her past life; something she rarely did these days. She was quiet by nature, and quieter still from having shared her childhood home with four loud and obnoxious brothers who overwhelmed her delicate sensibilities and caused her to retreat into her own world. Her job as a data entry clerk for a hospital suited her because she didn't have to interact with others. She stayed in her own cubicle, working with her head down, eating her home-packed lunch at her desk.

She had never had many friends, and she frankly preferred her own solitude; it was safer. At twenty-four she wasn't technically a virgin, but in spirit she remained unopened; sexually immature. Brian from work had been the one to take her virginity. They dated for only a few months. There was never any love, and very little passion. He was a decent fellow, though rather short, which Jane didn't like. In her mind, her "real" lover would be tall, as he looked down lovingly at her. But that was fantasy and Jane was a practical girl. She would take Brian, since he was one of only a few men or boys who had ever noticed her in the slightest.

Brian was very eager to consummate their relationship by having sex. He couldn't understand Jane's reluctance, it never occurring to him that he would be her first. Jane sensed that Brian was growing tired of her protestations, and she knew he would probably break up with her soon if she didn't let him have sex with her. Her instincts told her to let him go. She knew she didn't love him and was even more certain that he didn't love her. They were a convenience for each other; something to do. But a part of her was curious; she wanted to find out what all the hoopla was about.

And so, one Saturday evening when he made his overtures yet again after they returned to her small apartment from the movies, she didn't push away and say, "No, don't," when he tried to grab her breasts.

Emboldened, he had slipped his hands into her bra, roughly

tweaking and pulling at her nipples. She didn't stop him, though she wasn't especially forthcoming in her response. When he leaned down to unzip her jeans, she only closed her eyes, arching her hips slightly to allow him to pull them down. White cotton panties were eagerly pulled at by sweaty hands as Brian maneuvered himself over her.

She didn't ask about protection, though she knew she should. She didn't tell him she was a virgin, as she was more ashamed than proud of this fact, at the age of twenty-two. Averting her face, Jane gritted her teeth, and waited for the pain she was sure would accompany his amateur thrusts. Instead, she felt his hand, fingers wet with his own spit, probing, opening her, massaging the sensitive folds above her entrance. Startled by the zings of sensation his hand caused, her eyes opened and she saw him intent upon her. She blushed as her eyes were drawn to his groin, where his erection was ample evidence of his desire. She closed her eyes again as he massaged his own cock, rock hard, though not very large, and then she felt him press it against her, slowly at first, attempting to gauge her reaction.

It did hurt as it pressed in, but not nearly as much as she had feared. The initial slight tearing of flesh made her gasp and, afraid Brian would realize he was deflowering a virgin, she forced herself to smile at him. She moaned a little, like she thought she was supposed to. All of this was wasted on Brian, who was intent on one thing as he began to move, grunting a little as he shifted on top of her. It was over rather quickly. He kissed her neck for a few moments and then rolled off her, tucking his cock back inside his briefs, quickly zipping his jeans. He asked her if it had been good for her, and she assured him it had been wonderful. He didn't notice the smear of blood and she felt sure her secret was intact, even if she no longer was.

After that she felt more confident, and looked forward to their Saturday night date, which would invariably end with him quickly fucking her and then taking his leave. It wasn't that the sex was especially fulfilling; she never orgasmed with him—but she felt more like a woman. Someone wanted her at least, though she couldn't figure out why. After a few months, things petered out and she decided with her usual fatalistic sensibility that she didn't particularly care.

Jane was not a person in touch with her feelings. She pretty much let life happen to her and usually had decided in advance that it wasn't going to go her way and there was nothing she could do about it, so she would just get on with things and not think about it too hard.

Jane was not romantic. But still, there was a boy once, Tom Dillon, in twelfth grade, who had made her heart sing with desire, who had made her damp between her legs. They would kiss in his car until their lips were chapped and crashing together. She never let him go further, though now she wished she had. He was the boy she still thought of during those rare times when she masturbated alone in her efficiency apartment. He was the one she could orgasm to, but he was long gone. Her only true love, as she thought of him; but he too had grown tired of her. She wasn't cool enough or wild enough to suit him and he had moved on, leaving her heart broken and more closed and guarded than ever.

But the real reason she almost looked forward to sex with Robert was because he had told her it would be in his bed. He said he didn't want to fuck her in her room on the hard floor. He would take her in the master bed.

Brenda brought her there, her grip tight on Jane's upper arm as she steered her along the plush carpeted hallway. She pushed her along in front of her as they entered, and Jane suddenly felt like a concubine in some medieval tale being brought by the royal steward as an offering to the king.

Brenda forced Jane to kneel in front of Robert, who was lying resplendent in his hairy nudity atop the satin sheets, cock already in hand and hard as rock.

As Robert fondled himself, Brenda sat on the edge of the bed and reached out a hand to stroke his cock for him. They ignored the naked young woman at their feet for a moment. Jane dared to look around the room. It was beautiful, decorated in teal blues and greens. It was bigger than Jane's whole apartment!

Furtively she looked around, noticing a large low vanity of cherry maple with a huge round mirror set above it. Strewn casually over its surface were any number of beautiful pairs of earrings and glittering bracelets. One bracelet in particular caught her eye; it seemed to be encrusted with diamonds and rubies set in what must be platinum. It was the loveliest thing Jane had ever seen.

Her attention was diverted from the jewels when Robert said, "Come here, frog. It's your lucky day at last." He held out his hand, beckoning her to him and, knowing she had no choice, Jane rose and sat tentatively on the edge of the bed. She averted her face; even after all this time, she was uncomfortable and embarrassed to see Robert naked like this.

She was also very nervous, knowing he was going to fuck her now, and with Brenda watching and no doubt keeping a running commentary. Her face was impassive though, as she lay down at their command, barely taking up any room on the huge bed. Jane was finally beginning to learn to mask her feelings, her face as blank as a slate.

They were under the impression that Jane was a virgin, and Jane wasn't about to disabuse them. In fact, in spirit she *was* a virgin, having never been truly *claimed* by a man. Now she lay quietly, passively, waiting for whatever was coming. She had been training herself in relaxation techniques, though she didn't know that was what she was doing. It was really a matter of survival; of keeping her sanity in an insane situation.

She would mentally shut out what was going on; she would

leave, fly away as she thought of it. Her mind would zone out on what was happening to her body. She could still feel the pain, of course, but somehow she was able to control that edge of terror. She was learning to cope, she realized, with her bizarre situation.

She was a little frightened of Robert's huge cock, but less so than by a whipping or beating. At least a woman's body was made for this, she reasoned with herself. And she had been allowed out of her room and onto this heavenly bed! She had grown used to her hard, cramped little cage and could fall off to sleep with little trouble now. This bed seemed impossibly soft. The sheets were crisp and cool. A maid had probably put these sheets on just this morning, expertly tucking in the corners and then smoothing it down with a practiced hand. Someone who came into this house. Someone who obviously didn't know they kept a prisoner locked in a little room! Someone who might help her escape? Someone who might have her own set of keys . . .

Brenda snapped her back to reality by saying, "You're really lucky to get my Robert. He's the best. I only let him fuck cum-sluts like you because you're nothing more than dirt. A piece of ass for us to use and abuse. So, piece of ass, today Robert feels like fucking you. And I'm going to sit on your face and make sure you stay good and still for him."

Robert watched appreciatively as Brenda took off her silky gown, revealing her large well-shaped form. Brenda was a "real woman" in his estimation, not like this skinny kid they had abducted. Still, as slaves went, she *was* responsive. He dimly realized this was part of Brenda's particular ire against her. She was too sexual, though he didn't think frog even knew it herself yet.

Brenda straddled Jane's face and warned, "If you protest, frog, I'll put you *under* the bed for a week, with no food. And don't think I'm kidding." She shifted her weight, positioning herself so that Jane was pinned beneath her. Taking Jane's arms, she held them tightly at the wrists. Jane shuddered uncontrollably beneath her, but Brenda didn't care. Jane was just an object for their amusement.

Brenda looked over at her husband and said, "She's ready, darling." Jane's eyes were screwed tight and her mouth was bunched in an asterisk of protest. Brenda's heady musk pervaded her nostrils, as she squatted over the hapless woman, letting her private parts rest on Jane's upturned face. Jane believed her threat about going under the bed, and didn't try to move away, though she felt revulsion rising in her like a tide.

She was distracted by Robert, who straddled her lower half. She felt his thick, heavy fingers press inside of her. It hurt; she was dry with fear. He was patient, slowly moving his fingers inside of her and on her sensitive vulva, calming her, arousing her body even as her mind continued its silent protest. When he decided she was wet enough, he leaned over her, entering her slowly, pressing one thigh between hers, pressing her open with his long, thick cock.

Jane yelped as he filled her, her cry muffled by Brenda's pussy mashed against her mouth. The initial pain was soon replaced with a dull pressure; a fullness that wasn't actually painful, once her vaginal walls adjusted around the rock hard cock inside of her. Robert began to move slowly, taking his time. He paced himself, giving the girl a chance to adjust to each ratchet of intensity.

When he felt her yielding beneath him, he began to pick up the tempo, loving the feel of her impossibly tight pussy clenched around his cock. Moaning, he arched and thrust into her, getting a deep thrill from fucking another woman while his wife sat on her face, slowly grinding her pussy against the unwilling young woman who writhed beneath them.

For Jane something unexpected was happening. She had been waiting for the pain of his entrance, and then enduring the onslaught, praying for him to come as fast as possible. But instead, the pressure was somehow transmuting to a pulsing pleasure inside of her. If only this woman's cunt weren't covering her face, forcing her to breathe in the sexual fumes. Jane arched convulsively, her own body out of control as it responded to Robert's expert movements.

With a loud moan, he came hard into her, kissing his wife's mouth as he did so. Brenda bit his lip, hard, as she came from her own thrusting on poor Jane's mouth. Jane was nothing more than a fuck mat underneath the lovers. Her own impending orgasm was stymied; this wasn't about her.

When they finished with her, they pushed her to the foot of the bed and held her there with their feet. She lay still, her pussy sore, orgasm denied, body aching. But the bed was so soft! And the sheets were like silk caressing her bare skin. Amazingly, she fell asleep, right along with her tormentors.

It felt odd to be wearing clothing after all this time, however scanty. Just a few short weeks ago, being forced to parade in this getup would have thoroughly embarrassed and humiliated Jane. She realized dimly that something was wrong; that she was becoming too indifferent, too willing to obey every command with barely a thought about it. Her main preoccupation was with avoiding pain and getting food. Just like an animal. A part of her whispered, *wake up, Jane. You're losing yourself; they're winning!* But she was too tired, or too afraid, usually, to listen. She would think about it later.

Today she was dressed up like a cheap streetwalker. Black stockings and garters, high stiletto heels that she had trouble balancing in, black leather garters, and a black bra that was too big on her. Brenda had cut out small circles in the center so Jane's nipples were visible. She wore black crotchless panties. As a final touch, Brenda was applying heavy makeup. "Hold still," she ordered, as Jane wobbled on her heels. Brenda was carefully brushing on a thick smear of blue eye shadow. With eyeliner, mascara, deep red lipstick, and plenty of rouge, Jane looked garish and haggard. Brenda swept her hair up in a French twist, but tendrils of the flyaway uncooperative hair kept slipping from its pins.

Brenda stood back and looked her over. "Perfect slut," she said, admiring her own work. The contrast to her own subtly applied makeup and elegant silk pantsuit was lost on neither of them. Let Robert see quality and trash, she thought. He would choose the trash though, because he basically was a slut, too, but Brenda didn't mind. Let him rut with this whore and then sleep in *her* bed. She'd give him as many little sluts as he wanted. As long as the end of the day found him with her.

She nodded toward the camera in the corner of the room, certain that Robert had been watching the preparations. Sure enough, he came sauntering in a few minutes later. "Well, what have we here?" he asked, acting surprised. "Where did you pick up this two dollar piece of trash?" Brenda smiled with satisfaction and pushed Jane forward.

"Show him what you got, girl. And tell him how much you cost."

Jane turned around and bent over, as Brenda had instructed her to do. She pulled the crotchless panties aside to show Robert her ass and pussy. Then she said, "Five dollars, sir." Robert laughed, hugely enjoying the cruel joke.

"Five dollars! That's a rip-off! I won't pay a penny over two!" Fishing in his pocket, Robert actually pulled out two crumpled bills and threw them at Jane. She felt a creep of indignation but a look from Brenda sent her back to that dangerous zone of complete compliance.

"Here's what you're going to do, whore. You can have the money, but you have to earn it. You take those dollars and go to the wall there. You have to hold them in place with your forehead, while the john here does whatever he wants to you. If the dollars stay in place, you get to keep them. If they fall, you get a whipping. Am I understood?"

"Yes, ma'am," Jane nodded, bending down to retrieve the bills. Slowly she hobbled on the tall heels to the wall, the bills clutched in her hand. Dutifully, she placed them against the wall and then leaned her forehead against it. Maybe she'd get some food for this. She hadn't eaten yet that day.

Robert came up behind her. Reaching his arms around her, he tweaked her nipples and then twisted them till they stood erect. "Give me clamps, Bren," he said, and Brenda went to get the nipple clamps. Reaching around, he secured first one and then the other to Jane's nipples. They bit into tender fleshing, wrenching a gasp of pain from Jane. But still she managed to keep her head pressed against the wall. After a moment, her body was able to adjust to the pinch on her nipples. Robert took the chain between them and pressed it against her mouth. "Hold onto this with your teeth," he ordered. She bit down. What a picture she made, dressed in her garters and stockings, red nipples poking through the black leather, compressed by the wicked silver clamps, pulled up by the chain held in her teeth.

Robert pressed against her, unzipping his pants so he could free his ever hard cock. Because of her stiletto heels, he was at just the right height to fuck her from behind. Ripping aside the flimsy black fabric of her panties, he pressed a finger and then two into her cunt. Forcing the moisture with his skilled touch, he then put his cock at her entrance, and holding her, pushed his penis into her.

As he rocked her, she kept her head pressed to the wall, her entire focus on the dollar bills. "Such a whore," he grunted, fucking her hard. "Just wants her money. Do anything for the money."

To test her, Brenda called out, "What are you, frog?"

"Your worthless cunt, ma'am," Jane intoned, her voice flat, just as Robert came inside of her. Brenda stood back, a bemused expression on her face. He might be fucking her, but the slave belonged to Brenda.

Jane was on her hands and knees, with her forehead touching the floor. Brenda was standing over her with a whip in her hand. Jane hadn't had any food or water for close to twenty-four hours. She felt so weak she could barely concentrate on what Brenda was saying to her. Robert leaned against one wall, watching the proceedings, looking almost bored. He perked up when Brenda said, "Okay, now, cunt. I'm going to make you perform for your supper." Jane perked up as well. Food! Please God, let the crazy people feed her; she was famished.

Brenda went on, "If you follow everything I tell you to do, to the letter, I'll let you eat and drink until you can't eat another thing. Now. The first thing you have to do is spread your asshole for us."

Even as tired and hungry as she was, Jane felt a flush of embarrassment and anger at this absurd demand. But food! The promise of food! Reluctantly, but surely, she put her hands to her bottom and spread her own cheeks for her captors' amusement. Robert leaned in to see her degradation, his cock straining against his jeans. "Good slut," Brenda said, enjoying the thrill of total control over another human being.

"And now, stick your finger up your nasty little asshole." As Jane obeyed, her face burning with shame, Brenda began her lecture about debasement. "You see, Robert. When they get properly trained, and when they get hungry enough, they are all the same. Pride is stripped away in the face of fear and survival. No one is immune. Not the strongest, bravest man," she dug a toe into Jane's bony side, "or the most stubborn little cunt."

"What I'm really talking about here is being stripped of dignity. Stripped naked. It isn't just about being physically naked; it's about being emotionally bared—desecrated. It's an intensely powerful and intimate act. It's as if dignity were a shell or a wall; another defense, another barrier to intimacy and connection. You see, Robert," she went on, though he really wasn't listening, preferring to focus on the little tart fingering her own buttocks on the floor in front of him, "grace and composure and self-control are distancing devices, used to keep other people at bay. Jane here has no self-control left. No dignity. She is stripped bare. She is nothing but our frog, our slave, our piece of property to use or destroy as we wish. I'll prove it."

Brenda pushed at Jane with her foot until Jane fell on her side. She leaned down, forcing Jane to focus on her face, on her words. "Open your mouth, bitch. I'm going to piss in it. When I'm done, I'll bring you a steak and home fries and a huge glass of cold water. I'll bring you apples and apricots and some pastry. But first my piss. Go on, open wide."

Jane opened her mouth. Her degradation was complete.

Chapter 5
SEX—PROMISES AND THREATS

Jane was standing in the middle of her room. What morning was it? She no longer knew what day it was, though she could see daylight through her little window, and a dark black sky at night. Sometimes the night sky was so breathtakingly beautiful she almost forgot where she was. It would be dotted with thousands of tiny stars that looked like twinkling diamonds in a sea of black ink. She realized they must be far out in the country. No city lights competed with the blaze of stars. Jane could spend hours watching the heavens, sometimes sitting for so long that the black faded into gray and then pink. As the stars faded she would be painfully reminded of the glass and walls that separated her from the rest of the world.

Day blended and bled into night. Time was measured by when she got to eat, when she got to shower, when she was tortured, when she was left alone.

Today Jane's arms were extended, wrists shackled and pulled up, secured by chains that hung from the ceiling. Her ankles were similarly chained and spread so that she was forced to stand in a taut X. Her pale body was marked with long pink and purple marks from prior whippings. Her ass was bruised and blotched from a recent paddling. Each rib was etched under her almost translucent skin, round little breasts were pulled high by her raised arms, the little rosy nipples stiffening in the cool air. Her lank blonde hair was greasy, and there were bluish marks of fatigue smeared under each pale-lashed eye. Her mind was empty, her focus only on how to stand so as to cause the least discomfort while she waited for her tormentors to come to her.

Brenda had come in early, ordering Jane up and out in a crisp no-nonsense voice. Jane had climbed out of her cage, hugging her naked thin frame with her arms, waiting for Brenda's orders, her head down. Usually she was up before either of them came in, and could relieve herself in private. Last night she had been mesmerized by a meteor shower framed in the little square of her window. She hadn't returned to her palette until dawn.

When she heard the door being unlocked she was instantly awake, but lay still in her cage, waiting. She had hoped for Robert, with a tray of food. When Brenda came first, breakfast usually was foregone. She needed to pee, but didn't dare ask.

Without speaking, Brenda grabbed at Jane, pulling her arms up and securing each wrist, climbing on a little stepstool to reach the ceiling hooks. Today she used metal cuffs, which ratcheted tighter if the person wearing them were to struggle.

"Stand feet apart. Wider," she directed, kicking at Jane's ankle. Jane did as ordered, blushing furiously as Brenda casually grabbed at her pussy, fingering it, pressing inside of her. With one hand still buried in Jane's cunt, Brenda took the girl's chin in her hand and forced her face up.

"Robert's in the mood for a little needle play." Jane blanched. "He used to do tattoos when he was in the Navy. You like needles, frog girl?" Brenda smiled an evil smirk and pinched Jane's pussy lips with her long sharp nails. She didn't seem to expect a reply.

Releasing her hold on Jane's pussy, she busied herself securing Jane's ankles.

Needles! Jane hated needles. Beyond being whipped, being bound, even being caned, she was terrified of needles. She had always avoided shots at the doctor's office; even giving blood made her sick. Just the thought of the long thin sharp needle piercing her skin made her break into a cold sweat. She felt nausea rise at the thought that Robert was going to use a needle on her.

When Brenda was satisfied that Jane was secure, she left her there. Time became meaningless in the silence, and Jane closed her eyes, images of a life past floating in front of her. Parents she hadn't seen in three years. Brothers she never visited. Her little apartment with the red Formica kitchen table and chairs. The window she had always meant to put a window box on and fill with flowers. If she ever got out of here, she'd plant those flowers. Something bright and colorful. Jane whispered a prayer to nothing in particular. Then she fell silent, willing all thoughts out of her head.

After some time, perhaps ten minutes, perhaps an hour, Jane became increasingly aware of her bladder. She had sipped from her water bottle before Brenda had come to waken her. Now she regretted it. As more time passed, poor Jane began to fixate on her bladder. Her wrists ached, and she longed to close her legs. But more than anything, she needed to pee. Because her legs were spread, she couldn't use her muscles to hold back the urine. It was through sheer will that she didn't let go. Distraction arrived in the form of Robert. He was dressed in his shorts, his burly chest bare except for several thick gold chains, which to Jane looked tacky but were no doubt worth a fortune.

"Froggy!" he boomed, "I'm ready to play!" Jane choked back a sob of fear. Robert held out a small velvet box which he opened with a click. Inside were rows of long, thin, very sharp-looking needles. Robert extracted a small one and held it up for Jane to see. He grinned. "Brenda mentioned you looked a little sick around the gills at the mention of needles. Not to worry. I'm going to help you. I'm going to desensitize you. By the time I'm done with you, you won't even mind the sight of your own blood." Jane's head fell back and her eyes closed. She was as white as death, but she was still conscious.

Brenda came in to watch the show. It wasn't often that Robert engaged purely in torture. He was such a randy man; things usually always degenerated into a sex fest for him. But he *did* like needles. Robert showed poor Jane a selection of long thin sewing needles, ranging in size from one to three inches, of varying thickness, all with very sharp points. He took one out and held it between two fingers, bringing it close to Jane's face. He forced her to open her eyes.

"Please!" she cried, her voice cracking with fear, freezing in her throat.

"So now you're saying please! What a nice change. 'Please poke me with that long sharp needle,'" his voice pitched up in falsetto. "That's what you mean, isn't it, cunt? You want to feel it pierce your flesh." As he spoke, Robert came close to Jane so she could feel his breath against her face as he bent forward.

Instinctively she pulled back, trying to get away, but of course there was no escape. Robert dragged the needle lovingly down her cheek, using the flat of it, holding it parallel to her face so she only felt the cold metal, but no prick. Still she was terrified.

"Please, sir" she begged again. "Please, not that! Please!" She began to cry, little sniffling sobs, gasping for breath. Robert stood back, somewhat surprised by her strong reaction. After all she had endured, to react like this over a little pinprick! He didn't understand, but he smelled her fear, saw her terror. He felt his cock stiffen with pleasure as he watched his captive try to avoid the little point in his hand.

Gently he poked her right breast, just barely scratching her with it. Jane squeezed her eyes shut and again arched back. He took a thinner needle and pressed it against her soft flesh, breaking skin, watching intently as a tiny droplet of bright red blood appeared. Looking down, Jane screamed and began to babble, begging him to stop. She had jerked back hard, causing the metal cuffs to tighten, cutting into her wrists and ankles.

Robert appeared unmoved, but then his expression changed and a slow smile spread on his face. "Hey," he whispered, his mouth close to her ear. "You *really* hate needles, huh? So much you would do anything to get away from them. Am I right?"

Jane nodded fiercely, a flicker of hope lighting in her eyes; maybe there was a way out! For a price. Always a price, but one she would pay to avoid another prick of his horrible needle. "Please," she whispered.

"Well, not that I have to ask your permission for anything, whore, but I have this little fantasy in mind, and it involves Mistress Brenda here." Bowing toward his wife, Robert went on, "I liked seeing Mistress squat on your face. But you didn't seem that into it," he grinned, avoiding the obvious pun. "I like to see a little enthusiasm when girls play. I want to see you eat cunt like you like it. Like you live for it. I want you to show me what a slut cunt-lapping little bitch you are. I want you to convince me you *love* it! And if I don't believe you, then you get all these needles, every single one, stuck into your tits and your cunt. That's right, your little pussy will be all stuck full of sharp needles, like a pin-cushion! I'll tie you down on a table and give you some acupuncture that'll make you see stars." He paused to let the image sink in. "So, do we have a deal?"

Jane nodded, relief palpable in her face, not thinking about what she was agreeing to, but only that he was putting the needles back and shutting the case.

"Okay, then. You just stay here a while and cool your heels. No breakfast for you today. I want you to be hungry for pussy!" He laughed, pleased with himself.

As they started to leave her, still tether and chained, Jane managed to say, "Please, sir?"

"What?"

"Please, um, I didn't get to use the bathroom this morning and . . ."

"You never get to use the bathroom, you stupid cunt. You piss in the drain, like the filthy slut that you are!" Of course he knew what she meant but he enjoyed making fun of her, of watching the dull pink suffuse her features again and again. The girl was so thin-skinned it was ridiculous!

"I need to go," she finished, her eyes pleading.

"So go, who's stopping you? You're filthy anyway, what's a little more piss? We'll hose you down before I let you get near Brenda, so do whatever you want. Bye now." They left the room, shutting the door with a little click, leaving her there, naked and alone.

She held it as long as she could, hoping against hope they'd come back and let her down, but it didn't happen. In fact, they were watching her on the closed-circuit T.V., as they lazily ate their breakfast. The two sadists waited to see how long their prisoner would last till she peed on herself. They were patient and would wait as long as it took.

As it happened, it took about another half hour, and then with a long plaintive sigh, poor Jane let go, feeling the hot liquid dribble down one thigh, and then splash between her legs in a little yellow puddle. She couldn't even close her legs, but was forced to stand there, naked and in chains, urine dripping from her pussy, until her captors saw fit to release her.

Brenda came in eventually, and Jane opened her eyes slowly, feeling too weak and defeated to even wonder what was next. She was so hungry and her arms were asleep. When Brenda let her down, Jane slumped to the floor, landing in her own urine. "What a filthy pig you are," Brenda said. "You aren't getting anywhere near me stinking like that. You're disgusting!"

Tears welled in Jane's eyes, but she didn't respond. It was true, but obviously there was nothing she could do about it. Then Brenda spoke softly, her voice suddenly kind. "Would you like a shower, Janie? A real shower? A hot shower?"

Jane looked up at her, not sure she had heard right. Brenda was staring at her, clearly waiting for a response. Slowly Jane nodded, sensing a trap, wary. "And maybe some lunch after that? How about a hamburger and some fries?" Jane's mouth watered so much that she had to swallow repeatedly not to choke, even though she was pretty sure she was being set up. Again she nodded, feeling her empty stomach like a little knot inside of her.

"Well, what would you give for it?" Ah, the trap was being sprung. What would she give? As if she had a choice in the matter. She would *give* whatever they took. That was how life was, her life. There had been a life before, but it was dim now, in the constant blaze of fear and survival which had become her world. She waited for the shoe to drop.

"No, I'm serious," Brenda said, as if she really wanted an answer.

"I don't understand," Jane said, her voice hoarse with disuse and thirst, remembering belatedly to add, "ma'am."

Brenda let the little slip pass. "I was thinking you might like a shower and a good meal. And I know Robert wants you to kiss me," Brenda's euphemism for pussy eating. "See, the thing is," Brenda paused, as if thinking how to phrase it. "The thing is, I know you're straight, and scared of pussy. I know you don't want to do it. I know you will, of course, because you have no choice. It's just that, well, I want you to," she paused, trailing off, looking away and Jane realized with a shock that Brenda was embarrassed! How could that be? And yet there it was. "I want you to want me," she whispered softly.

Jane didn't respond. She was confused and didn't really understand what Brenda was asking. Her own sexual experience was so limited, it didn't occur to her, not on any intuitive level, that a woman could desire another woman. Brenda waited another moment, and the sudden vulnerability in her face was replaced by a hardening anger. She mistakenly thought Jane was rejecting her offer; rejecting her. Jane had no clue of what Brenda might be feeling, but she saw the change in expression and knew she had lost whatever chance she had had.

"Fuck you, bitch," Brenda spit out. "Robert warned me not to expect anything from a frigid idiot like you. Fuck you!" She flounced out, taking the fleeting dream of a hot shower and food with her.

The spray was cold and would sting against recently whipped skin. Robert attached the long green hose to the spigot in the wall near her pee drain. He attached a spray nozzle and ordered Jane to stand over the drain, hands behind her head. Jane stood as ordered, shivering in anticipation of the cold spray. When it hit her body she gasped at the force of it, at the coldness of the hard water.

Robert soaked her, spraying her body, her legs, her head, leaving her spluttering and spitting as the water dripped from her hair into her eyes. Brenda, standing nearby, was ready with a bucket of soapy water. She took a rough cloth from the water and scrubbed on Jane's body, rubbing methodically, leaving Jane's skin pink and soapy. "Spread 'em," she said, pushing against Jane's thigh. The heat of a blush licked at Jane's neck and face as Brenda roughly scrubbed at Jane's pussy and asshole. She dipped the washcloth and washed under her arms. Then she squirted some shampoo into her hand and massaged it into Jane's scalp.

"Do it yourself," she ordered, allowing Jane to massage her own head and hair. Despite how cold she felt, Jane was so glad of this chance to wash. Her head was itchy with oils and dirt from not having been allowed to clean herself.

Gratefully she massaged her scalp, even as her body shivered uncontrollably from the dripping water. A final rinse and Robert tossed her a towel. Jane dried herself quickly, careful on the various bruises and welts which always marked her body from recent beatings.

Brenda left the room as Robert stood watching Jane dry herself. As she tried to comb her hair with her fingers he said, "That's good enough. Let's go. And remember, I want you to enjoy this. Brenda's pussy is some of the finest around. I want you to lick it and suck it just like I do to you. And you'd better make her come, frog, or you'll still get the needles. And that, baby, is a promise."

Jane entered their bedroom in front of Robert, who gestured toward the bed where Brenda was reclining. She was dressed in a lovely dark green silk nightgown that had a long slit up the front. She was propped on many pillows, and her legs were lewdly spread. "Come to mama, little slut," Brenda smiled in a way that was meant to be sexy, but which held nothing but menace to Jane.

She was being ordered to make love to another woman. She could do this, she told herself. It was easier than taking a beating or being fucked in the ass! And it had to be worth it to avoid the dreaded needles. Still, she found herself feeling squeamish. Brenda was a large woman, and her large hairy pussy looked ominous to Jane. Robert gave her a little push and Jane crawled forward on the bed, marveling silently anew at the softness of the sheets and the inviting give of the mattress.

Hesitantly, Jane knelt between Brenda's ample thighs, not sure what to do. Brenda gazed down at her and looked to Robert. He smiled back at his wife and pressed Jane's head down toward her pussy. Brenda hiked her nightgown and shifted herself so that her pussy was now directly in Jane's face. Jane held her breath and bent down. She was trying to get up the nerve to "kiss" Brenda when she felt her head jerked roughly back by the hair.

"Got a problem, frog?" Robert said harshly. "My wife not good enough for you, huh? Now do it like you mean it, and don't forget my needles!" He let go of her head suddenly and she fell forward, losing her balance for a moment, her cheek brushing Brenda's thigh. Flustered, Jane righted herself and again leaned between Brenda's spread legs. This time she gingerly stuck out her tongue and touched Brenda's pussy.

The scent of musk and sex assailed her nostrils. Holding her breath, Jane closed her eyes, moving slowly closer. She licked the outer folds and Brenda sighed happily. "That's it, froggy, that's it." It wasn't so bad; a little salty but not bitter like Robert's semen.

With surprising gentleness Brenda guided Jane's head, positioning her and pressing against her to encourage her kisses in just the right spots. Jane began to lick and suck in earnest, as Brenda responded with her moans and movements. Encouraged by her fear of the needles and also emboldened by Brenda's response, Jane put a hand on either thigh to get better access to her sex.

She remembered the movements and techniques Robert had employed on her and tried to imitate them on Brenda. It seemed to be working, as Brenda sighed and her breathing quickened to a pant. Robert sat near them, his huge cock in his hand as he watched his naked prisoner lick his wife's cunt.

Something strange began happening to Jane. She wasn't crazy about licking another woman's pussy, but she found that she got a little thrill from the responses she was drawing from Brenda. This woman who had tortured and abused her for so many weeks was now writhing and moaning under her tongue and hands. Jane was the one in control! Jane had the power to make this woman respond and she liked it!

She continued to kiss and lick her, even daring to press one finger into her sticky entrance. Brenda bucked into her hand when Jane did this, crying out, "Yes! Yes!" And then she shuddered, holding Jane's head tightly against her, fucking herself against Jane's tongue and mouth, her vaginal walls clamping on Jane's finger as she reached her climax.

At last she let go of Jane's head and Jane drew back a little, feeling a secret triumph, though not quite daring to wipe her wet mouth and face. "Good froggy," Robert patted her head in a gesture which secretly infuriated Jane, but she only bowed her head, keeping her eyes down. "Now you can sit quietly on the floor. Don't move. You can watch me fuck my wife. She seemed to like what you did. So no needles *today*. Not yet." He laughed cruelly, pulling Jane to the floor and ordering her to stay still as he climbed onto his wife and rutted with her in front of their slave.

"Hold yourself open. And don't move. And don't whimper. Not a sound." Jane was on her hands and knees on the floor. Robert was crouching behind her, cock poised at her pussy. When she didn't instantly obey, he grabbed her by the hair, pulling her head up sharply. "I said hold yourself open! Reach around and spread your pussy for me. You know you want it, slut. Now *do it*." He accented the words by pushing her head roughly forward.

Now that she had been introduced to the supposed wonder of his cock, with all the fanfare in his bed, fucking Jane was a daily event.

A vasectomy several years back prevented that annoying inconvenience of getting his sluts pregnant. Not that he bothered to inform them; why tell an object anything at all? Except when you wanted something from them. They existed solely for his pleasure. It was that simple in Robert's terribly twisted mind.

Leaning with her shoulders against the hard wood for balance, Jane reached back with trembling hands to open herself for Robert's rape. "Look at you," he sneered, pretending disgust though he was deeply excited by her display. Her dark pink pussy looked so pretty all spread and open for him. "You're just dying for me to rape your little cunt, aren't you? You're just dying to feel my cock in your little twat. Now remember. I'm going to fuck you now, and I don't want you to move. I don't want to hear a sound out of you. You move or cry out, and you'll be punished, don't think you won't," he said, guiding his penis into the pussy held spread by the slave's own fingers. It felt so good; she was so hot! She may be ugly, but her pussy was so tight!

He wanted it to last. He moved slowly, letting her adjust, noting with satisfaction that she was staying still and staying quiet. She probably liked this, the little whore. Who wouldn't love his huge dick inside them? He didn't care how much these little cunts protested; he knew deep down they all wanted the same thing—a big dick buried in their nasty little snatches. He began to thrust more savagely, irrationally almost angry with Jane for pretending to be such a frightened virgin, when they both knew she really wanted it. Voicing his thoughts Robert grunted, "You *want* this, don't you, frog? You *want* my cock in your nasty slit." He thrust hard, punctuating his words with his cock as he slammed into her. Jane jerked forward, crying out as he hurt her, hands flailing as she tried to keep her balance.

She failed, falling to the floor, and Robert landed on top of her in an ungainly heap. "Bitch!" he shouted. "I told you not to move! Get up!" Miserably, Jane tried to get up, but he still lay on top of her. Wrapping his powerful arms around her, he rolled them both over so that she was straddled on her back on top of him, his cock still inside of her. He lifted and lowered her for a moment, like he was doing exercises, and her body was the dumbbell. Then he lifted her off and said, "You blew it. Your cunt isn't good enough for me now. I'm going to take your ass. Get back on your knees."

"Please, please, no," Jane started to beg. He had placed her on her hands and knees. Now he crouched behind her and wrapped an arm around her neck, pulling back hard. The pressure was tight against her throat and Jane couldn't breathe.

He hissed in her ear, "Don't you *ever* say 'no' to me again. Do you understand? *Ever.*" His cock was pulsing with need now. Jane's face was red and her eyes were bugging out. She looked hideous. He let her go, and as she gratefully gulped in air, he spit on his cock to lube it up. That's all she was getting today, the little bitch. Holding her tightly by her hips, he guided himself into her ass, ignoring her cries for mercy. If anything, they made him harder. It was over too soon, and he came with a loud moan into her, grabbing her tits, twisting and pulling her nipples as he slammed his body into hers, causing them both to fall again to the floor. This time he didn't berate her, but simply pulled out of her and left her in a tangled heap.

Her ankles ached and her head throbbed from the pressure of being upside down. She kept wanting to reach her arms out to steady herself, but of course she couldn't. They were bound tightly to her sides. Today Brenda was using something she had had special made for her binding games. Heavy strips of fine cotton had been dyed a deep, blood red. She kept these strips, great mounds of them, in a large sewing basket, pulling out varying lengths as it suited her needs and perverted pleasure. The strips were soft but strong. At least they didn't rub and burn Jane's skin the way the nylon rope did when it was tied tightly.

The young woman presented quite a picture, hanging upside down from the ceiling, her entire body trussed in vivid red, except for her ass, pussy and tits, which were conspicuously bare. She hung by her ankles, which were secured in thick leather straps that were attached to short sturdy chains hanging from the ceiling. Robert had cleverly designed the pulley mechanism so that Brenda could secure Jane in the straps while she was lying on the floor, and then slowly ratchet the chains up until Jane was suspended, just by turning a large wheel on the wall.

Brenda had wisely tied the girl first, so that she wouldn't flail and make it too difficult to get her into proper position. The frightened little bird had offered barely a protest as Brenda had knelt, lovingly tying the knots that bound Jane's arms completely to her sides. She wrapped the red strips around and around, starting at her feet and not stopping until even Jane's face was covered in red, only nostrils and lips showing.

Now she hung like some painted mummy, her sexual parts exposed and waiting for whatever fiendish tortures they had devised. As Brenda turned the wheel, spreading poor Jane's legs even further apart, she asked, "Comfortable?"

Jane could hear her, though from her position sound was obscured by the sound of blood rushing in her head; it actually reminded her of the seashore when she was a child. She would find shells and hold them to her ear, and then take as many home as she could fit in her sandy lap, squished between her brothers in the sticky backseat. She tried to let her mind go there now—to the seashore, where the waves lapped peacefully against the sand.

A long low whistle interrupted her brief reverie. Robert had entered. "Wow, Bren, she looks like those Japanese chicks who get off on the rope thing! I *love* how you left her cunt and tits like that. Yum, they look like candies that have just been unwrapped! And I've got a sweet tooth!"

Brenda smiled, also quite pleased with the effect. She sat back now, hiking her little denim skirt so she could get a hand on her own bare pussy. "Come here, baby. I need you." Brenda's voice was husky with arousal. Bondage always got her especially wet, and the frog looked so hot with her cunt and ass exposed and her whole body tethered in the beautiful red rope. Brenda wasn't looking at Robert as she spoke to him; her eyes were fixed on the slave girl. Robert approached her, and she pressed him down till he was kneeling in front of her. She hiked her skirt so her bare cunt was exposed and commanded, "Lick me."

Robert's eyes were bright with lust. "Oh, yeah," he said, "oh, yeah, baby." Eagerly leaning forward, he spread Brenda's solid thighs with each large hand, bringing his mouth to her pussy. She was aromatic with desire and he inhaled with pleasure as he tongued her.

Jane was swinging slightly, her body slowly twisting in its rope and chains. Brenda grabbed Robert's head and gyrated her hips into him, breathing hard. She came fast, her eyes glued to the young woman in the blood-red bondage. Without ceremony she pushed Robert back from her body. He sat back, grinning, his face wet with his own saliva and her juices. Wiping his mouth with the back of his hand he said, "Done already? You must have been aching for that one."

Brenda smiled sheepishly down at him. She had been so horny it hurt! That one little orgasm had only just taken the edge off. But now it was Robert's turn to do as he liked with the slave, and Brenda knew it would be good.

First he took a large vibrator and lubed it up. Jane's legs were spread so that her pussy was easily accessible. He pressed the hard plastic phallus against her lips, easing in the tip, pressing it until he drew a grunt from the girl, who tried, unsuccessfully, to close her legs. He slid it in as far as he could and then flipped the little switch at the base, letting it buzz into life.

Brenda licked her lips, wondering if she should go get her own personal vibrator to use while she watched the fun. But she didn't want to miss anything. Slipping out of her clothes, she licked her fingers and settled back. As always, using the ropes had gotten her beyond hot.

Robert looked over at Brenda and said, "The butterfly?"

"Sure, why not? She's been a good girl." Brenda was feeling expansive. Robert got the little soft plastic attachment that slipped over the vibrator so that it was resting, like the little butterfly it was named for, directly on Jane's hooded little clit. The frog jerked slightly and Robert could see she was feeling it.

He smacked her ass several times, watching the creamy white skin turn pink and then red, his hand prints showing against it where he struck. The force of his blows made her sway. Still the vibrator whirred inside of her, the little wings of the butterfly stimulating her against her will.

Robert moved down to her tits, kneeling in front of her to get a good angle. The bright red ropes were wrapped around and crisscrossed between the perfect little globes. They looked like pink-tipped snowballs against a red landscape. Luscious. He took one nipple in his mouth and pulled and licked it until it hardened. It felt so good, like a little soft marble in his teeth. He moved to the other and bit and kissed it, laughing softly as the slut's nipples responded.

Brenda rubbed herself, moaning slightly. She wanted Robert's mouth on *her* tits, but she knew her time would come soon enough. She loved watching him wrench a response from the unwilling little cunt. And he was. Despite being hung upside down, bound, and immobile, Jane's body was being affected by the relentless purr of the vibrator filling her pussy, and the butterfly tickling her clit. Her nipples, extremely sensitive, responded of their own accord to Robert's expert ministrations.

She was breathing hard, but otherwise silent. Confusion over this unwilling sexual pleasure and her hapless condition was again reigning in her troubled mind. It was too hard a fight; she let go and just *felt,* not thinking, not anticipating what pain would surely follow the pleasure. She just let go.

Robert, unaware, or at best indifferent to whatever Jane might be feeling at the moment, was pulling his own cock out of his shorts. He stood behind the tethered woman and pressed his body against hers, holding her still in his arms. "Come here, baby," he gestured to Brenda, who stood, hand still caught in her panties.

She joined Robert, standing in front of Jane, so that they sandwiched her between them. Leaning over her pussy, between her legs, they kissed, both rubbing their bodies against her. Brenda locked Jane's heads between her knees as she leaned forward, her tongue in her husband's mouth. Jane could feel Robert's hard cock pressing into her back. It felt like a steel rod, rubbing up against her as he bent forward to take his wife's nipples into his mouth one by one. Brenda moved around and took her husband's cock in her hands, her long fingers curling around it as she moved herself into position to take him into her throat.

They sank to the floor next to Jane, oblivious of the fact that the vibrator was still whirring in her pussy. Robert positioned his wife on her hands and knees, doggy style so they could watch Jane while they fucked. When she began to moan, her body spasming with the shudders of an orgasm she couldn't control, Robert slammed into Brenda, his balls slapping her ample ass.

"Do it, baby!" Brenda screamed, wrapping her arms around Jane's legs to steady herself as she came just after Robert did. Still the dildo vibrated inside of poor Jane, whose body was jerking and twitching. She was screaming now, a high pitched little wail filtering through the cloth that covered her mouth. The sound finally pierced the cum-soaked consciousness of the two tormentors. Robert, as usual, was the first to take pity. Disentangling himself from Brenda, he stood and flipped of the switched.

Jane's body still twitched and spasmed for a minute or two after, the nerve endings still over-stimulated from the sexual torture. She longed to close her legs, or better yet, slip away into unconsciousness. That didn't happen, but mercifully she felt herself being slowly lowered. The wheel was being turned and then strong hands cradled her head as she was laid out on the floor, still bound head to foot in blood red rope.

Sharp steel scissor blades slipped between the bonds and her sweaty skin, slicing the strips of cotton from her body. Jane shivered as the cool air touched her fevered skin. She was soaked with sweat which immediately began to dry, wracking her body as she shuddered from the sudden cold. She was too spent even to open her eyes as she felt strong arms lift her and settle her into her cage.

Then the room was blessedly silent. She was alone again. How much longer could she go on? For just this moment, she wished she could slip away forever; just disappear, washed gently into the sea that still lapped at her consciousness. She drifted into troubled sleep, the waves in her dreams carrying her into a warm oblivion.

Chapter 6
NEEDLES

Each day, unlocking the door, Robert snapped his fingers, which Jane had come to understand meant she was to get out of the cage and stand at attention in the middle of the room. If she didn't move fast enough, he would push her down to the ground and soundly whip her ass and thighs with his crop until she was on fire. Then he would order her back up into position. She would stand, again lacing her fingers behind her head, tears spilling down her cheeks, biting her lips to keep from crying. Robert didn't mind when she cried; actually he liked it.

But stubborn Jane didn't want to give him the satisfaction. She rarely got whipped anyway now. At least not because of not being in position. She was nimble and she would be ready to jump up when she heard the key in the lock. She slept as lightly as an animal, always wary, always on the edge of dreams, waiting for the nightmare of her reality to snap her into consciousness.

Today he had a new game for his captive. "I've never seen you play with yourself, frog." Jane said nothing as she scrambled to attention in the center of the room, fingers locked behind her neck. Robert came close, standing directly in front of her. "Lay down, pussy girl. Show me what you used to do in your crummy little apartment all by yourself when you were dreaming of me but didn't know it yet." Jane dropped her head, looking up at him in an effort to be coy. When she played along he treated her much more gently. She felt like a prostitute when she did this, but better a whore than a whipping post.

Carefully she lay down on the hard floor, awaiting further instruction. Robert had seen every detail of her body so intimately she found herself somewhat inured to his probing eyes and fingers. Still she flushed when he commanded, "Spread your cunt so I can see it. Hold it open for me." It was one thing to be "done to," but to be ordered to handle herself in this way, in front of him, embarrassed and humiliated her.

"Do it," his voice was hard now and she knew she risked a beating if she hesitated any longer. Slowly she reached down and spread her own pussy lips, turning her head in shame and closing her eyes. "Look at me," he ordered. "And smile."

She opened her eyes, staring up at the brutal man kneeling next to her. Barely concealed hatred blazed out of pale blue-green eyes while her mouth tried to smile and effectively only grimaced. Robert didn't notice. He was looking at her cunt, at the pink folds spread for him with long thin fingers. Leaning over her, he bent down and licked the folds, wetting both her fingers and her pussy lips.

"Now you do it; I want to see you cum, little whore."

Jane closed her eyes again and began to move her fingers. There was no way she could orgasm by her own hand in front of this man. She would have to pretend. Would she convince him? She rubbed herself and tried to move her hips in what she hoped was an erotic way. She moaned a little and rubbed faster. She felt nothing.

"Yeah, baby," he whispered. "Do it. Do it for me." Robert sat near her, his own cock out, stroking it to erection as he watched

Jane touch herself on the floor. But now he really looked at her face, at her lips pressed together in concentration, at her eyes screwed shut. She was rubbing and moving and making little gasping sounds. There was a rhythm to it that was almost mechanical. The bitch was so obviously faking it that it was pathetic.

"Okay, you can stop now, frog. Since you can't cum for me, you're going to suffer for me." Jane stopped, dropping her hand, her expression one of resignation and defeat. She felt so tired lying there; she wished Robert were a bug so she could squash him. The image almost made her smile, but it was whisked away by his next words.

"Spread those cunt lips again. But this time I'm going to whip it. I'm going to beat your nasty little pussy for not doing what I told you to do. You deserve it; you know you do."

Jane said nothing, but did as he ordered, knowing it would be worse for her if she dawdled. Robert took his little crop and knelt between the naked woman's thighs, forcing her legs far apart. She was trembling, but still holding open her sex for his promised torture. Thinking of Brenda's methods, Robert said, "Count for me; let's see how high we can get before you pass out."

Smack! The crop hit her tender flesh and Jane screamed. But still she managed, "One!" He smacked her pussy again and again, beating her cunt with the little leather loop until Jane fell out of position, covering her sex with her hands, trying to avoid his blows, no longer focused on obeying.

"Move your hands, bitch," he yelled, slapping them away with the crop. She tried to comply and tried to count but finally her body took control in its effort to protect itself and she curled up in a ball as his crop hit all parts of her, leaving little red squares of stinging pain. At last Robert dropped the crop, breathing hard with exertion. He stood up and stared down at the young woman still curled in self-defense.

"Brenda would flay you alive for that, frog. You're lucky she's not in here. I'm gonna go eat something, but when I come back we're gonna move to tit training. And I'm gonna tie you so tight you ain't going nowhere. Cunt." With that parting epithet, Robert turned on his heel and was gone.

Jane lay still in a fetal position, arms wrapped around her knees, quieting herself. Slowly she crawled to her cage and pulled the little door shut, wrapping herself in her blankets. Her whole body was stinging from his cropping, most especially her poor pussy. How much more of this could she take before she lost her mind? Sometimes she wished she would lose it. She wished she would just leave her senses and become a robot that had no feelings and no dreams.

She lay hugging herself and thought about this, realizing with a little shock that she was glad she was "still here" in spirit. As horrible as it was to endure the daily torture and confinement, she was still alive, and she hadn't given up hope. The old Jane would have despaired and resigned herself to certain death. But somehow something seemed to have been forging in her spirit over these weeks of hell—a will not only to survive but to live, to escape, to be free. She didn't know how she would do it, but the new Jane would never give up.

These brave thoughts were wiped away as the door opened and both her tormentors returned. Brenda had the dreaded coils of rope in her hands. "Get out of there, cunt," Brenda said brusquely. "You're going to be punished." She didn't know the specifics, but Robert had told her that Jane was disobedient and needed to be punished. Brenda was only too glad to comply. It was she who suggested the needles.

Jane slowly stood, knowing she daren't defy these two. She felt fear prickle in her scalp and drag through her innards like ice and fire. She was right to be afraid. Brenda tied Jane's wrists and elbows tightly behind her, forcing her breasts upward and forward. As

Robert held her from behind, Brenda wrapped the ropes expertly around each breast, forcing it up and out, compressed and distended from her body. The ropes were tight and made her breasts ache as blood was trapped. They traded places and Brenda stood behind the bound woman and wrapped a strong arm around her neck, keeping her still in a chokehold.

"We'll start with your tits," Robert casually informed her, as he pulled a long thin sewing needle from a little packet he had in his pocket. Jane's eyes widened with terror and her face went white with fear. Slowly, his face alight with sadistic pleasure, Robert brought the sharp point of the needle to Jane's right nipple. Brenda clenched her tightly from behind as Robert pricked the nipple with the silver needle. Jane screamed and struggled but Brenda was very strong. "Ah," sighed Robert, and he pricked the other nipple. Little droplets of bright red blood appeared at each nipple. The pressure from the ropes caused the blood to flow more freely. Lovingly, Robert leaned down and sucked the nipples, while Jane squirmed and cried. It was too much. She passed out, falling limply back against Brenda.

Robert got a stool and they lifted the still unconscious woman onto it. Leaning her back against Brenda, Robert pulled Jane's legs apart so that her sex was exposed to him. Brenda waved the smelling salts he handed her under Jane's nostrils until Jane stirred and opened her eyes. She saw Robert in front of her, his body between her thighs, preventing her from closing her legs. Brenda held her still from behind as she rested on the stool, still bound with rope.

Robert brought the needle down to her pussy, his cock impossibly hard as Jane screamed with terror. He poked her delicate flesh while she writhed, her strength surprising Brenda, who wrenched her arms back to keep her still. Jane sagged suddenly, a blessed swoon claiming her yet again. Brenda was tired of this game. "She's out, Robert. Let's take a break. She's worthless right now."

• • •

The days passed, with sexual pleasure and torture following one after the other, melting into Jane's exhausted and frightened psyche, leaving her with few thoughts but how to survive each ordeal, and how to survive for one more day in her personal hell. She always tried to obey every command with alacrity and respect, hoping it would earn her some modicum of trust and perhaps win her the occasionally promised privilege. They had taken to leaving her cage door unlocked at night unless she was being punished. She would often get out and exercise, or just wander the room, stopping just under her little window, staring at the lone patch of sky which was her only connection to the outside world. If she were left alone, she would watch the clouds drift, or the sun pass by, and dream of times when she was free, and could step outside whenever she wanted. She would return to the cage to sleep though, shutting the little door, as if she could somehow keep the dangers out by doing so. Ironically, her prison became her safe place.

In the many hours she spent alone musing, Jane realized that she had never really lived her life at all before. She had spent her time being bitter because others didn't like her, or didn't know her. She had really been sleepwalking through her life, going through the motions, never truly experiencing anything. She had never appreciated her job, her apartment, the food and drink she could freely eat whenever she was hungry, the ability to take a walk when she wished, to use the bathroom, to see a movie, to listen to music, to read a book, to drive a car, to sleep in her own bed. She vowed to herself that if she ever got free of this horrible place, she would cherish each and every moment of her life. She wouldn't worry about her looks, or her lack of friends. She would *live* each moment as if it might be her last.

Chapter 7

GIRL-GIRL PLAY

"Get up. Today's a special day, frog. Hurry and pee, and then stand ready for your shower." Jane climbed stiffly out of her cage and went to the drain, squatting obediently, peeing in front of Brenda with almost no embarrassment now. She was focused instead on the word *shower*—her entire body itched with dry sweat and the secretions of others. She stood almost eagerly, awaiting the cold spray of water that she knew would refresh her, once she got over the chill. Brenda tossed her some soap, and Jane lathered up as best she could while Brenda lazily aimed the hose at her. Too soon, Brenda tossed her a towel and said, "Today you get to meet someone new. You are *not* to talk to them; not a word. If you do, I swear to God, this will be your last day on earth. This is a friend of ours. She likes girls and she's very, very good.

"Robert thought it'd be fun to watch her engage in her particular blend of pleasure and pain. And consider yourself lucky. There are people who pay good money to have done what Suzette is going to do to you. Good money. Robert and I will be there the whole time. One slip, one hint that you're our prisoner, and goodbye life. Is that clear?"

Jane nodded, confused, her heart pumping with the thought of someone new. Surely this person would know something was amiss? Surely she would see the crisscross of faded and fresh welts, the bruises, and the look in Jane's eyes? What if she discovered something without Jane saying a word? And then Brenda blamed Jane and decided to kill her anyway? Jane began to breathe too fast, and felt faint. Please God, don't let her die today. As horrible as this life was, she found she still wanted to live it. A spark of realization awoke in her suddenly, making her remember things that the constant barrage of torture and denial had made her forget. A little voice whispered inside of her—*there is a life other than this.* She might still find a way to live it.

Once her body was dry and her hair combed, Brenda blindfolded her and tied her wrists loosely in front of her. She was brought to a different part of the house. She could tell it wasn't their bedroom. The bed here felt different when they helped her to lie down on it. Where was she? Who was this Suzette she was to meet? Jane's senses were alert now; alive with not only fear, which was a constant, but with curiosity.

She knew better than to ask. Patiently she waited for whatever was to come. She heard them talking in the hall and then the tinkle of feminine laughter outside the door. It opened and she heard, "Jane, this is Suzette. Suzette is a good friend of ours. She knows we sometimes have *friends* like you come over to play." Jane sat numbly on the bed. Surely this woman wouldn't believe such a story.

Brenda had turned to Suzette. "Jane here is a little new to all this, but she is a total submissive and a pain slut. You can see by the fresh whip marks, she likes, no, she *craves* the whip every day. Just the type of girl you like to play with and use." Brenda's expression was one of a queen bestowing a gift on one of her noblemen.

Suzette was about 5'7" with dark hair pulled back in a clip at the nape of her neck. Her makeup was flawless and accented her large almond shaped eyes, which glittered against lovely coffee colored skin. She was dressed in a Chanel suit, with Italian pumps. A thin gold choker accented her long slender neck and the matching stud earrings hung elegantly in her lobes. She didn't look the part of a dominatrix, but more like a model, an investment banker, or an attorney. Of course Jane, blindfolded as she was, couldn't see Suzette.

"Aren't you going to take that thing off?" Suzette asked. Her voice was low and seductive, with the hint of an accent, maybe French or Haitian.

"No!" Robert answered quickly. "It's part of her training. Her master gave her to us on loan. He doesn't want her looking at anyone but him until she's properly trained." Brenda smiled at Robert, as if to say, "good one." She further embellished the story.

"That's right. He wants her to learn about pain and pleasure. About how they can mix and heighten the experience. And you, darling, are a queen of pleasure and pain, as we well know."

Suzette ducked her head modestly, clearly pleased at the compliment. She had evidently bought their story, every word. Jane realized with a little shock that there must be whole worlds about which she had no idea. Worlds with masters and slaves and training techniques. A world where bound and blindfolded young women were an everyday affair, and she was nothing out of the ordinary. Should she try, though? Cry out to this woman that these people were *not* her friends, but her jailers? Crazy, dangerous people who had abducted her and who knew how many others?

She started to speak; she had to try, even if it meant death. "Please, you've got to-" She was cut off by Brenda's hand clapping over her mouth. "Slave!" she screamed in Jane's ear. "You forget yourself! Your master expressly forbid you to speak! He would *kill* you if he found out that you disobeyed him! He warned us of your insubordination. Robert! Quickly. Get the ball gag and gag the slave. Then she'll be soundly punished, don't you agree Suzette?"

To their guest, this was all just a delicious game, and Brenda was playing her part beautifully, as was this young slave girl. Too thin, but she had potential. Suzette liked her mouth; there was an unexplored sensuality there. "No," she put a hand on Robert's arm. "Not the ball gag. It is so *gauche*, darling, don't you think? I am sure little Jane here will promise to be quiet, won't you, dear?"

Miserably, Jane nodded, thoroughly defeated. She had tried to speak and now she knew not only that she had failed, but that Brenda would probably kill her for it. Literally. She fell back on the bed, almost paralyzed with fear. "There," Suzette soothed, smiling at Brenda. "She will be a good girl now, I think. But you are right, Brenda. She must be punished. What does she hate the most?"

"The cane," Brenda promptly replied, feeling somewhat appeased since Suzette had asked her advice.

"Ah, the cane. Most brutal. I don't usually use it myself, since the marks can be permanent. I prefer my girls unblemished. But I can see from this one's skin that her master has no such requirements. Very well, then. The cane it shall be. And then the rubber strap on her bottom. I do like the rubber strap."

"Get on the floor, frog," Brenda ordered, pulling Jane roughly to her feet. Jane stood, and felt her shoulders pushed down so she was kneeling. Her head was pressed until her ass was raised. Robert knelt in front of her and stretched her arms out, holding her wrists against the floor in one hand.

"Frog?" Suzette was curious. "Why do you call her that?" Brenda was holding the long supple rod of bamboo, fingering it lovingly. She seemed momentarily flustered. She had meant to continue to call Jane by her name, or "slave" as if she were really someone else's girl.

"Oh, ah, just a nickname her master sometimes uses. Affectionately of course."

"Hm," responded Suzette thoughtfully. "Well, it doesn't suit her. Not at all." Jane, head down, heard the remark and it eased the tiniest part of her knotted heart.

It was forgotten, though, when Brenda brought the cane down with a slicing of air and caught her just below her ass, on her upper thighs. Jane screamed and Brenda caught her again in the same spot. "That will teach you to speak out of turn, slave girl! Now be quiet and take it! You know you love it." Tears wet her blindfold and Jane bit her lips till they bled, trying to keep from sobbing. Brenda wanted to whip her more, but she felt Suzette's cool fingers on her arm, restraining her. This was, after all, only a game to Suzette.

"Let me show you what this lovely little strap can do," she said, showing them a piece of rubber tubing about half an inch thick and 12 inches long. The real beauty of this is the humiliation. You make the slave bear themselves, and then you whip their little asshole with it. It's a very sensitive area, you know, and you can effect quite a punishment without marking your property at all. Especially good for the paying customers I have; the judges and politicians who are cheating on their wives and can't be marked." She smiled serenely, and said, "Spread your asscheeks, little Jane. I will introduce you to the pain of the strap, and then to the pleasures of my tender ministrations."

Robert let go of Jane's wrists, and she slowly reached her hands back to spread her cheeks. She was whimpering softly and her thighs were on fire. As she bared her asshole, Suzette brought the rubber hose down, striking her in that tender place. It felt like bees stinging her all along her crack. She cried out and Suzette said, "You deserve this, my petite. But don't worry, it will soon be over." She struck the poor girl another five times and then brought the rubber hose to Jane's trembling lips. "Kiss it, darling.

I like for my slaves to kiss the object of their punishment." Jane pursed her lips, trying to kiss the hose. She managed to brush her mouth against it, which satisfied Suzette.

"And now, my love, your reward for being so brave. I do men for money, but girls," she paused as she slipped out of her Chanel suit, easing it to the ground. "Girls I do for free." She stood, magnificent in a white satin bustier that showed off her size C breast, the silky cloth only barely covering the dark brown nipples. She wore tiny panties that showed most of a completely shaven pussy. Brenda and Robert both sighed with appreciation. With her lovely olive complexion and smooth shapely body, she was truly extraordinary.

Suzette helped poor Jane up and gently directed her to lie back on the bed, on her stomach. Jane's wrists, still loosely shackled, were over her head resting against the headboard. With a delicate tongue, like a cat, Suzette licked the thin red welts along her thighs. It stung at first and then soothed her. Suzette gently parted Jane's ass. Jane clenched her buttocks uncontrollably, but Suzette whispered, "Stop, darling. Relax. Remember your master's desire that you be trained to be with a woman." Of course there was no such master, but still, Suzette's soft touch and tender tone allowed Jane to relax to some degree. She felt Suzette's fingers gently probe her bottom. She jumped slightly when she felt Suzette's tongue there. But it felt good. So soft and soothing after the painful whipping with the hose. Suzette licked her ass, and then moved up her back, long fingers smoothing and massaging her shoulders.

"This girl is too skinny," she announced to the others. "Tell her master to feed her better."

"Oh, she's anorexic; he says he can't get her to eat!" Brenda responded, irritated that Suzette kept finding critical things to say. Maybe it wasn't such a good idea to bring her over. Robert, as usual, wanted to watch a show, and Suzette *was* good once she got going . . .

Suzette nodding understandingly and then returned to her charge, strong fingers relieving tensions that had stayed with Jane since her abduction weeks ago. She sighed a little with pleasure as Suzette deftly smoothed and kneaded knots of tension from her neck and shoulders. When Suzette pressed on her side, wanting her to turn over, Jane complied. Suzette touched one of Jane's breasts, remarking, "Jane, these are truly lovely! Definitely your best feature! They are so beautiful! The perfect size and shape. And those luscious nipples, like little cherries just waiting to be tasted!"

As soft hands caressed her, the tiniest smile appeared on Jane's lips; so unused was she to a compliment. Brenda and Robert had her convinced she was the ugliest thing on the planet; and already having believed herself plain, it hadn't been hard to do. Now she felt Suzette's mouth against one nipple. Not the rough licking and biting she experienced at Robert's hands, but a gentle swirl and tease that made her arch slightly, though she didn't realize it, for more. But Suzette realized it; she could sense Jane's responses intuitively, however guarded the young girl appeared to be. There was something very odd about this one. But then, Brenda and Robert were very eccentric. And despite her comment about doing girls for free, they were in fact paying her very handsomely for this particular meeting.

So she focused on the task at hand, making dominant but tender love to this slave girl, and giving her benefactors a good show. Having stimulated and aroused Jane's breasts, building up a pleasure in her belly that was evidenced by her erect straining nipples and the suffusion of color on her cheeks, Suzette did her classic switch, and slapped one breast hard, drawing a cry from Jane. Then the other breast got the same treatment. A true masochistic submissive, such as Suzette was used to dealing with, and such as she had been led to believe Jane was, would have been further aroused by this rough treatment.

She bent down to kiss Jane, expecting an ardent kiss in return. Instead she was greeted with a closed mouth. Hm, perhaps this girl was not "into girls" as it were. No matter, Suzette would bring her around. She tried kissing her a little more and then slid down to Jane's pussy. Slowly she forced Jane's legs apart, kneeling between them, her own ass raised prettily in the air. She licked the sensitive folds delicately, like a cat tasting cream. She felt Robert come up behind her, his large hands on her ass. Normally Suzette didn't allow anyone watching to touch her; it threw her off, but he had paid her well for her time, so she decided to let him make the rules for now.

She licked, kissed and suckled Jane's pussy until Jane began to writhe on the bed, trying to close her legs. Of course Suzette wouldn't let her, and she kept on kissing and teasing her, now inserting a slim finger into her vagina, feeling the hot wet walls clamp around it. She smiled; even the shyest girls were no match for her skilled tongue. Robert's erection was pressing hard against her through his pants. When she felt him stand back and heard him unzip himself, Suzette shifted position. She didn't want to be fucked by this guy, however much he was paying. He had bought a girl/girl show and that's what he would get.

She moved up to straddle the blindfolded girl's face. Jane's nostrils were assailed with her sex. She felt Suzette's soft labia brush her lips and nose. They were smooth as a baby's, freshly shaven. The scent was not heavy like Brenda's musky folds, but a lighter, more delicate fragrance, like fresh rainwater with a hint of apricots. Jane knew what was expected, and oddly, she almost wanted to lick this woman's pussy. She had been right on the edge of an intense orgasm, something she rarely experienced either before or during her captivity. She had wanted it, even if it was in front of the captors; she had wanted to slip over that lovely edge. To experience something pleasurable after so much torture and pain.

Maybe if she returned the favor, this Suzette, who was at once so gentle and so rough, would do it again. So she opened her mouth without being ordered to do so, and snaked out her tongue. Suzette settled her weight, holding herself up slightly so Jane could reach her inner folds with her tongue. Jane began to lick and tease her, mimicking what Suzette had done to her. She found herself wondering for a second if this made her gay—in that she didn't absolutely abhor what she was doing; she even kind of liked it. She didn't dwell on these thoughts; there would be ample time to think later when she was locked back in her prison.

Something of the old spirit started to seep back into her soul, as she realized the lesson again which she had been just beginning to learn—we have to live for the moment, because in the end that's all there is. If this were her last night on this earth, she would take what she could from it. She focused on kissing Suzette's pussy, noticing when she moaned or shifted to give Jane a better angle to do what pleased her.

Jane felt Suzette's fingers reach down and begin to caress Jane's sex. She let her thighs fall open, oblivious to Brenda and Robert's leering eyes, wanting Suzette's touch again. Suzette's fingers tapped out a sweet dance on Jane's pussy, matching her own tongue's rhythm against hot moist flesh. They moaned together, moving inexorably down a path toward intense release. All of Jane's defenses were down, due to exhaustion and the constant underlay of fear, yes, but also due to something else. This skillful lover on top of her was not only bringing Jane to orgasm, but using Jane's lips and tongue for her own pleasure. Again Jane felt the thrill of power over another person's pleasure, but more than that, an actual joy and pride that she could draw those cries and mews of pleasure from another. They came together, with Suzette's fingers never stopping, even as she ground her pussy against Jane's mouth, shuddering and shivering against her.

Ever the dominatrix, she slapped Jane's cunt with a flat hard palm just as Jane's spasms of pleasure were subsiding. Jane cried out in confusion, the pleasure blending into pain once again, leaving her completely undone.

The next day found Jane bound, naked of course, to a high bar stool. She was bent over it, with her wrists and ankles secured to the legs with white nylon rope. The rope burned her skin if she pulled against it. The blood had rushed to her head and her ass was raised up, splayed and inviting the torture that was about to be visited upon her. Robert and Brenda were both dressed in tight black leather pants. Brenda wore stiletto heels and Robert sported soft leather boots. They were both topless.

"You know you're going to get punished, don't you, frog?" Brenda glared at the girl, clearly expecting a response.

"Yes, ma'am," Jane managed to answer, her mouth dry with fear.

"I had much worse in mind, but Robert here convinced me that if we use you up too quickly, there won't be anything left. Then we'd have to find a new cunt to torture. Which would suit me fine, if you want to know."

Jane believed her, absolutely. She also believed that that was the time they would kill her. She felt panic rising like a tidal wave in her and a little cry escaped her lips.

"Shut her up, Robert! I don't want to hear her whining tonight. We should have gagged her before we let Suzette near her. I told you that! Now, gag the bitch." It wasn't a request. Robert did as she demanded, buckling the bright red ball gag into Jane's mouth, his expression almost apologetic. He knew what was coming, though Jane did not.

They stood on each side of Jane, with long tapering red candles in their hands. Robert lit Brenda's and then his own. "Ever had a hot wax treatment, frog?" Robert asked, of course knowing the answer. Jane was in no position to respond. She jerked when the first hot splash landed on her ass. They both held their candles over her, watching her jerk as the hot wax elicited muffled moans and cries from behind her ball gag. They covered her back, ass, and thighs in burning little blobs of red wax.

Brenda looked grim. This girl could have really blown things for them and she was still angry. She was no where near finished with this little bitch. "Take out her gag; I want to hear her scream."

Robert unbuckled the contraption and Jane drew grateful shuddering breaths, barely registering what Brenda had just said. Her back and ass were literally on fire, covered in a myriad of tiny burns from the melted wax.

Robert blew out his candle and set it down. He had participated in this punishment before, and knew what Brenda expected of him. A large hand on either asscheeks, Robert spread poor Jane's asscheeks, giving Brenda a perfect target of her little tight asshole. Brenda let the first drop fall against the tender opening. Jane screamed, her cry shrill and high. She jerked hard against the tight ropes and rocked the stool. Robert put a hand on her back to steady her.

"Take it," hissed Brenda, and dropped another molten red drop of liquid on her asshole. She covered Jane's asshole with wax, which hardened into a covering. Jane was screaming all the while. Then, with a nod from Brenda, Robert untied the tortured woman and lay her down on the floor.

"Now listen, bitch. I'm going to burn your cunt. And I want *you* to hold it open for me. And I want you to beg for it. Come on, girl, let's hear you beg for me to drop this wax on your nasty little twat."

Jane was crying softly, and struggling with the dizziness caused by the blood rushing back to her head from being released. With trembling fingers, but knowing she had no recourse, Jane spread her pussy lips, gulped, and whispered, "Please, Mistress, please burn my pussy with the wax."

"My nasty pussy," Brenda amended.

"My nasty pussy," Jane confirmed, her voice cracking.

Robert held her legs wide while Brenda straddled Jane's waist and let the hot wax sear her tender sex, drop after drop of hot wax burning her pussy till she passed out from the pain.

But still Brenda wasn't satisfied. A spray of cold water brought Jane to, and then Brenda told the dazed girl, "Now, it's your big mouth that got you in this trouble, so I'm going to give you one final wax treatment. I'm gonna seal your mouth with wax. And next time maybe you'll think twice before you open your trap."

When Jane next awoke from a swoon, she was where they had left her on the floor. Her hand flew to her mouth, fingers pulling at the cold wax that covered her lips and chin. Wax had hardened into little scabs all over her body. She spent the next several hours trying to peel it off her tender burned flesh. It would be weeks before all traces were removed.

Chapter 8

JEALOUS LOVER

Brenda was gone for the day clothes shopping and Robert had the little frog all to himself. Robert had found himself thinking of Jane more and more lately. Of being with her alone, without Brenda's watchful and jealous eye on them. He did love the torture, the humiliation, the control they exerted over their prisoners, but, as odd it might seem, he was a romantic at heart. He secretly found Brenda overbearing at times, with her constant need for his attentions. She *seemed* to be into his playing with other women, as long as he didn't show too much actual interest in them as anything more than pieces of ass. If he slipped up in the slightest, she would get her panties all in a bunch and it would take days to allay the jealousy.

He put up with a lot from her, and admitted to himself that it had more than a little to do with money—hers—which was all bound up in trust funds that would dry up completely for him if he were to leave her. Not that he wanted to *leave* her. He really did love her. And where the hell else could he find someone as twisted and perverted as he was? Someone who lived for the thrill of the abduction and torture of their prisoners? And who took care of all the messy details like getting rid of them when it was time.

But something about little Jane. He realized to his own surprise that he had just used her name in his mind, instead of his usual derisive frog. He liked to watch her blush with shame when he taunted her. But at this particular moment, he was feeling tender. She really wasn't that ugly; she just kept herself all closed up. She made ugly faces. Maybe if she were treated with love she would respond, like a real frog in a fairytale, and he would be the one to free her. No, that was stupid. He wasn't going to free her. But he could make love to her. Especially today, when the cat was away . . .

He entered her room, not seeing her at first, just a little bundle hidden in her blankets, safe in her cage. He came closer and knelt down. She jumped up, sleep blurring her features. It was rare to catch her sleeping; she was usually as wakeful as a little ferret, ready for their approach any time of day or night. She tried to scramble out of the cage and stand naked and at attention, as he had taught her, but he stopped her.

"Hey, cool it. It's okay. I don't need you at attention right now, little frog. I think I want to take you to my room. Just you and me." Jane stood up, hugging her thin body protectively. He led her out of the prison and down the hall on the carpet which was so thick her feet sank several inches at each step. She could sleep there on that rug and be in heaven.

He led her to the bedroom where he had fucked her while Brenda masturbated on her face. She was nervous and afraid, her body tensing for whatever new torture they had devised for today. As they entered the room she looked quickly around. Where was Brenda? As if reading her mind, Robert volunteered, "Brenda's gone shopping. We have the whole day to ourselves. Just you and me, Janie girl."

Janie? He never called her by her name. It was always "frog" or "cunt" or "slut" or some other derisive and insulting term designed to degrade and humiliate her. But instead of comforting her, his use of her name, of a diminutive of her name, somehow made her even more nervous. This man was crazy and she was totally at his mercy.

He led her past the bed to the large master bath. It was huge, larger than her bedroom in her former life. He led her to the large marble Jacuzzi which was already filled with foamy hot water. Steam was rising from it and it smelled wonderful, like freesia and sandalwood. He climbed in first, after stripping naked in front of her, completely unselfconscious. He held out his hand and Jane took it, climbing into the fragrant glorious water.

It swirled around her, warming and easing her always taut muscles and aching bones. The rushing water stung the myriad of little abrasions and welts from the constant beatings, but it was a good sting, and ultimately soothed her flesh. She felt as if she could melt it into it. She fantasized for a moment of just slipping under, breathing in and never coming up. But of course, even if she were the suicidal type, which she was not (being too stubborn), her captor would never allow it.

She was drawn out of her reverie by his question, "Champagne?" Robert was turned from her, opening a little refrigerator that was neatly placed in the wooden panels that surrounded the Jacuzzi. Such luxury was beyond anything Jane had experienced, or even thought about. She nodded, though she rarely drank. Still, she knew she liked champagne, having had it at various weddings and other festive occasions back in that distant life before now.

Robert popped the cork with a flourish and poured the champagne into two beautiful crystal flutes. Jane took the glass, which felt so delicate she was afraid it would break in her hand. She brought the bubbly liquid to her mouth and sipped. Ambrosia. It was delicious. Without meaning to, she drained the glass in a gulp. Robert laughed and poured her another.

"Go easy, frog, you'll get tipsy." He took out some cheese, already prepared in little squares, and some crackers, from the little fridge and set them between himself and Jane on the ledge. She looked at him questioningly and he nodded. Gratefully, she took a piece, wondering who had prepared the cheese. Who chilled the champagne? Had they any idea what was hidden behind the door at the end of the hall?

She ate as much cheese as she dared, and drank the three flutes of champagne Robert offered as if they were water. She was indeed rather tipsy, and the hot water was making her positively dizzy. Her face was flushed and her hair was wet from the steam and her own alcohol-induced heat. Robert poured some of the water over her head and then proceeded to gently wash her hair, as if she were a child. It felt so wonderful, so different from the cold needle spray they usually hosed her down with. What was happening? Was he going to kill her? Was this her last rites? Her last supper? Well, if so, this was a better way to die than she had envisioned at their hands. She let go her worries; she quashed her fearful fantasies and just closed her eyes, giving herself up totally to the wonderful feeling of food in her belly, warm water swirling around her, strong hands massaging her scalp, and champagne making her giddy.

Rinsed clean, she let Robert half guide, half lift her out of the tub. She teetered for a moment and actually giggled. "You *have* had too much," Robert laughed. He noticed she looked actually pretty when she smiled. He had never seen her smile before, but then, why would he. If he had had a conscience, it would have pricked him fiercely at that moment. But Robert, like Brenda, was one of those odd people entirely without a conscience. He had no empathy for others; he was incapable of understanding that others had feelings. He simply lived for his own peculiar pleasures.

And today his pleasure was to take this little woman to his bed and fuck her. Slowly, like a lover, not a slave. And no Brenda to order him around, or to intervene, wanting his full attention on her. It was barely noon, and Brenda had gone into the city. She had only been gone for thirty minutes or so. It would be hours before she returned. He smiled and said to Jane, who was wrapped in a thick white towel almost as big as she was, "Lie down." He pulled her down next to him on the bed.

She offered no resistance, and didn't try to cover herself when he removed the towel. She was too skinny; he would feed her, but first he would fuck her. And he wanted her wet this time; ready for him. No rape today. Skilled at the art of arousal, he began slowly, kissing her neck and gently massaging her shoulders. His fingers swirled down to her breasts, which really were lovely. He teased and pulled the little pink nipples until they were erect. Still dizzy, but so warm and comfortable in his bed, Jane felt his tongue flick against first one tip, and then the other.

Why resist? If she were to die, or if she were to be put back in the cage and tortured for another lifetime, she was here now, in this soft bed, with a man who was behaving like a lover instead of a monster. She would seize the moment and live for this very second. What else, after all, was there?

She smiled again, the champagne easing her inhibitions as he suckled and teased her sensitive breasts. He liked her responsiveness, and focused on her nipples, making her moan. Then his hands trailed down to her little pussy. He teased it with the lightest touch, like little butterflies. She sighed and let her legs fall open. Robert moved down now, putting his mouth to her sex, bringing her to the edge of release and then withdrawing, until she was fairly begging for orgasm.

Only then did he mount her, carefully, as if she were china, slipping first only the head of his massive cock into her opening. She was wet! Wet and actually eager for the penetration. *Fuck me,* she thought, though even now she dared not speak. Who knew when this lover might disappear and the tormentor re-inhabit his body?

But her body language was clear, and he knew she wanted him. Another few moments of teasing her cunt with his cock and then he thrust in to the hilt, drawing a grunt of pleasure as he filled her.

Now he fucked her hard, all his pent up desire slamming into her. He crushed her with his body, completely claiming her, riding her to his own orgasm, and, amazingly, to her own. She came as he did, feeling a hot, fierce pleasure clutching deep in her belly, wishing it would never end. He moaned and became rigid for a moment, holding her so tightly she couldn't breathe. Then his body relaxed and he fell against her, slumping into post-coital relaxation.

If only Brenda hadn't forgotten her charge cards.

She was standing in the doorway, staring down at the two lovers, her face grim, eyes glittering with barely suppressed rage. As Robert rolled off of Jane he saw her. He sat up suddenly, looking guilty, and then quickly trying to cover it with jovial nonchalance. "Brenda! You're home early! Join us, darling. I was just warming up the slut here, so she can kiss you properly."

Brenda cut him off. He wasn't fooling anyone, and he knew it. "Save it, lover boy. I wasn't born yesterday. I know you better than you know yourself. Don't get up. I only came to get my cards. I'm leaving again." She turned her venomous gaze to Jane. "You," she spat, "You I'll deal with later. Whore."

Jane was led back to her cage by Robert, who left to accompany Brenda to the city, hoping to make it up with a romantic dinner and carriage ride. Jane didn't know they were gone. She only knew that the champagne had worn off instantly when she saw Brenda looming in the door, as did the endorphins of pleasure resulting from the first orgasm from intercourse she had ever experienced. She was locked into her cage this time, and she had curled up into herself, trying to calm her tumultuous thoughts. Brenda was going to kill her; she felt fairly certain of this.

She had been aware of the little jealousies before, though they were completely unwarranted, of course. Who would ever be attracted to scrawny, frog-faced Jane when they could have statuesque and regal Brenda? But Jane realized that the heart was a strange thing. She didn't know much about relationships, but it was clear there was something up between these two, and she was definitely a focal point.

She pondered her imminent death. She wanted to be at peace with it. To die with grace and dignity. But she didn't think she could. She knew Brenda would torture her first; torture her until she died. *Oh God, stop it! Stop it!* She ordered herself to let it go. If she were going to die, so be it. We all die at some point. She could have been killed the first night they abducted her. She had expected it. Instead somehow she'd hung on for days, weeks, perhaps it was even months; she didn't know any longer. Eventually she drifted off to sleep, too dazed to even dream.

Her eyes flew open some hours later when she heard the door unlock and open. Brenda came in, alone, as Jane had feared. Robert would not be there to protect her; to distract Brenda, to keep her from going overboard. No, this was it. "Get up," Brenda said. She wasn't dressed up in any leather getup today. Just a white blouse and blue jeans. Work clothes.

She had a hand truck, onto which was strapped an odd looking chair. It looked almost like those old electric chairs you saw on T.V., with all the straps and handles. No, it couldn't possibly be that. Jane watched as Brenda pushed the chair into place on the floor and moved the hand truck out of the way. "Sit down," she said. Trembling already, Jane sat on the chair, wondering if she should try to fight Brenda; try to escape. But what was the point? The two of them could snap her neck as easily as look at her. She sat passively, waiting for death, a strange peace settling over her.

Brenda strapped her arms to the arms of the chair, tying them tightly with the large leather buckles over her forearms. There were stirrups for her feet, and Jane obediently put hers in them. Brenda strapped her in and then cranked them so that her legs were forcibly spread apart. Next she strapped Jane's neck against the back of the chair, sliding the strap through the holes made just for that purpose. She pulled it tight, completely restricting Jane's head movement. This last action cost Jane her self-control. Until then she had been almost in a trance; expecting the worst, relieved in a way that it was finally happening.

But something about having her head and neck restricted like that. Feeling the thick leather strap pressing against her trachea and knowing if she strained against it she would choke herself made her perversely do just that. Adrenaline pumped through her like a drug, leaving her breathless and tensed.

Jane was breathing hard, certain she was going to be tested beyond anything that had happened to her before. Usually Brenda chatted with her, explaining what she was doing, why she was doing it, or what she was going to do next. Brenda liked to use her words to titillate herself, to control her charge, to heighten the torture by creating anticipation. This new silence was ominous in itself. Jane didn't know what to expect. So naturally she expected the worst.

Brenda brought out the cane. It was long and supple and left angry welts wherever it was applied. Jane stiffened, her breath catching in her throat with an audible little yelp. Without warning, Brenda brought it down on her inner thigh. It hit like a searing flame. Jane screamed. Brenda smiled, and it did it again, to the other thigh. Then she stopped. Jane strained against her bonds, even though it was useless.

"Thank me."

"Thank you, Mistress," Jane gasped.

"Ask me to do it again."

"Please. I can't, please." Brenda brought the cane down on Jane's breast. Jane hissed her agony, but was completely immobilized by the thick leather straps which bound her.

"You can do whatever I tell you to do. Husband stealer. Now, beg me. Beg me to lash your cunt with the cane."

Jane tried. She knew she had to obey or it would be worse. But she couldn't bring herself to ask for the cane. She was too terrified to even form the words. They were frozen in her throat. "Worthless cunt," Brenda snarled, and brought the cane down on Jane's spread pussy.

When Jane came to, she was still bound in the chair. Brenda was standing near her, greasing up a huge dildo. "Took you long enough. Don't think you'll get out of anything by fainting. You like big cocks, so here is your own personal cock, bitch." Brenda shoved it into Jane's opening, ramming it in none too gently, tearing the flesh of her entrance. She fucked her for a few minutes, sliding it in and out, in and out. Jane was dazed, frightened, and still smarting from the caning. She couldn't believe this stupid woman actually thought she coveted her husband. The man who had kept her confined in a tiny room and tortured her—why in the world would she want such a man!

But Brenda wouldn't believe her protestations; Jane instinctively knew this. She tried to focus through the pain of the huge dildo ramming into her pussy. She had to come up with something to stop Brenda from flaying her alive. Even to buy herself another hour, another minute. "Please," she managed, between vicious thrusts, "I'm so sorry, Brenda. It'll never happen again . . ."

"You bet it won't. I won't be leaving you alone again with my Robert," Brenda snapped back. But she removed the dildo, seeming slightly mollified by Jane's admission of guilt. "You've earned this punishment, haven't you, frog?"

"Yes, Mistress," Jane nodded, ducking her head submissively.

"And you deserve to be caned, don't you?"

It took all her self will, but Jane managed to croak, "Yes, ma'am."

Brenda smiled with triumph and then brought the cane down on Jane's tender nipple. Pain blazed through her like fire and she literally saw stars in front of her eyes. The other nipple received the same treatment and Jane passed out again. When she came to, Brenda was unbuckling the straps that held her so tightly in place. She turned the cranks that released Jane's legs from their stretched positions.

Jane fell forward and Brenda made no effort to catch her as she slumped to the floor. Brenda had let her out of the chair well before Jane had thought she would. She knew she should be grateful, but she also knew Brenda wasn't done yet.

"Lick my boots." Jane was weary and she felt all the welts on her body like lines of fire. Somehow she forced herself up to her hands and knees. She moved herself to Brenda's right foot, which was indeed clad in a lovely, soft-black-leather boot.

Gingerly, she stuck out her tongue and licked the leather. Brenda lifted the shoe, offering the sole of it for Jane to do her duty. Jane licked it, trying to apply herself so Brenda wouldn't suddenly kick her. Brenda watched with satisfaction for several minutes as Jane covered first one sole and then the other with her tongue.

Pushing Jane back with the toe of her boot, Brenda snarled, "You are scum, frog. Get up and assume the position. I'm not quite done with you." Jane stood, barely able to keep her balance, exhausted from pain and fear. Brenda used the dreaded cane again, this time on Jane's back and ass. Jane fell forward on the ground, beyond revival this time, her back covered in a crisscross of oozing welts.

Robert found her where she had fallen and knew Brenda had gone too far this time. He cleaned the wounds and carefully laid Jane in her cage. He left provisions—fruit and cheese, crackers, bottled water, candy bars. He also left a tube of Neosporin for her to use on her welts.

This wasn't working out so well anymore, he decided. Next time they would get a guy. That should keep Brenda happy. She was so damn jealous! On the one hand he liked it; it meant she cared. But it did get in the way when he wanted to mess around with the prisoners. Distancing himself from Jane with these thoughts, he stood, satisfied that he had taken care of her sufficiently to keep her alive and usable for the next time. That, after all, was all that mattered, wasn't it?

They basically left her alone for several days, which suited Jane. No torture, no forced sex. Robert did come in once a day to remove any waste and leave something for her to eat. Maybe they would forget about her, and leave her to starve to death in her prison. Jane felt listless and defeated; what did it matter? Now or later, what was the difference?

As she began to feel physically better, she berated herself for this attitude. The welts were healing well. She had torn some strips from her blankets and had even dared to wet them in order to wash the wounds and keep them clean. No one came in to punish her for using the spigots; maybe they weren't watching her anymore.

She liberally applied the antibiotic cream several times a day. Eventually she got up and started to do her exercises again. She could at least keep up her strength. She ate all the stale cookies and other food she had stashed, along with whatever Robert brought her. She sang songs to herself, trying to remember the words to all her favorite tunes.

If she ever got out of here, she would spend an entire day just listening to music. She would learn to play an instrument. She would go to concerts. She would read literature, not just the fashion magazines and romance novels that in the past had always ended up making her feel bitter about her own wretched and lonely little life. She would get out and meet people! Maybe make some actual friends. She would join clubs for activities that interested her, like gardening and maybe even scuba diving!

She realized with a start that she was lonely, even for Robert. Not for Brenda. Never would be soon enough to see Brenda, but Robert had been tender with her. Robert had been kind to her. Robert had made love to her. She missed him, in a strange way.

When he came in the next morning she tried to engage him in conversation, something she never did. He seemed surprised to hear her speak. She was usually little more than a toy to him; a doll to play with in his own perverted way. Today she spoke, saying, "Good morning, sir. How are you?"

"What? How am I?" He stared at her for a minute. She was kneeling submissively in the center of the room; she had been waiting for him. "Oh, I guess I'm fine. How 'bout you, frog?"

"As well as can be expected, sir, thank you for asking." She wanted to say more, but didn't know what to say. She tried, "I really appreciate the food and what you do for me," she flushed slightly, thinking about the waste removal which still humiliated her so.

"Oh, sure. No problem. Listen, I really can't stay. Brenda's got breakfast going and . . ." he trailed off, glancing at the ever-present camera in the corner. Jane realized that of course he thought Brenda was monitoring them through the closed-circuit T.V., and of course, she probably was.

Jane bowed her head, hoping she hadn't earned another visit from the vengeful wife. She didn't try to stop Robert as he set her food down and disappeared, locking the door behind him.

Chapter 9

JANE

Robert came in carrying two large grocery bags. Jane looked up and then away again, afraid some new and terrible instruments of torture awaited her inside those bags. But in fact there was only food. Robert looked troubled, but he smiled at her, though it didn't reach his eyes. "Frog, we are going away for the weekend. Here's some stuff to eat and drink. We won't be coming in for a few days, but guess what? I've even slipped you a magazine. And here's a disposable container for you, ah, for when you 'use the bathroom' as you like to say."

Jane was stunned. Going away for the weekend? Two whole days without the tormentors? And a magazine! Something to read! How she hungered for something to read; something to stimulate her bored and tortured mind!

"Oh," she breathed, without stopping to remember she wasn't to speak until spoken to. "Oh, thank you so much! A magazine! Thank you, thank you!" Robert smiled benignly, like some king bestowing a fortune on his subject.

"Well, don't go counting on it happening again. We'll be back in two days. Behave yourself, and we'll, uh, see you when we get back." Robert turned away, something almost like sorrow flashing over his features before it was swallowed in his callousness. Had Jane known where they were going, she might have died simply from fright. They were going to bring their favorite hit man from the Bahamas to take the prisoner out. Usually Brenda went alone. But this time she said she was afraid of terrorists. They both knew the real reason was Jane. This would be her last weekend alive, if they had anything to say about it, and they had plenty.

And then it happened.

As he turned to leave something fell from Robert's pocket. It fell just as he was shutting the door, so that the click of the lock obscured any sound of metal hitting wood. Jane sat very still for several moments. He did not return. She stared at the little pile of silver and gold fallen by the door. Still she didn't move. It was as if time had slowed, or even stopped. She wasn't sure she could get up. Her legs felt like jelly and her heart was pounding like a freight train in her ears.

The keys. He had dropped his keys. The keys to her jail? She didn't know, but she was going to find out. Prayers began spilling from her lips, sent up to a god she didn't even know she believed in. She sidled toward them, and her hand shot out. Snapping them up, she hurried to her cage and hid them among the old smelly blankets. Forcing herself to be calm, she sat quietly against a wall and laid out the provisions the jailers had so thoughtfully provided her. Thank God for Robert. Brenda would have starved her to death by now, she was certain.

The food that he had left her normally would have sent her into spasms of ecstasy—there were plums and grapes, a loaf of bread, and a jar of peanut butter, a six pack of Dr. Pepper, a large bottle of spring water, two packages of cookies, and a package of salami. *Food of the gods,* she thought, smiling. But who cared! She had keys!

Jane forced herself to wait. She waited for a good half-hour past when she heard them leave and heard the car drive away, crunching along the graveled drive. She kept expecting Robert to retrace his steps to find his keys. But somehow luck stayed with her. She remembered the one time she had been in their car, it was Brenda who had driven. Perhaps Robert hadn't even missed his keys yet.

She waited just a little while longer, for good measure. They seemed to be well and truly gone. Gone! And she had keys! She silently admonished herself. They might be keys to his club, to his fishing tackle box, to anything other than her prison. She was foolish to let this rising hope pound through her veins like wine.

Well, she would stop hoping, stop wondering, and get up and find out. She fished the keys from their hiding place in her cage and went to her prison door. There was a car key, yes, definitely. And a two little keys that must fit boxes or something. And two more keys that looked like door keys. She tried the first one. No, it wasn't right. Damn. "Please, God, oh please, oh please, oh please," she begged aloud. She tried the second one, her hand shaking so hard that she was forced to hold it still with her other hand to get the key into position.

She felt as if her heart were literally breaking—the key didn't fit. None of the keys fit. She slid down against the door and sobbed until her tears dried up and nothing was left but dashed hopes. She looked up at the patch of sky outlined in the square of her little window. It was growing dark. She was alone in her prison with keys that didn't free her. All she had was a view out her window. Her window.

The words seemed to split and splinter in her mind, as if she were having a hallucination. She heard the words, slowly intoned, *the window*. The window. The small keys. One of them might— she didn't dare finish the thought. For several moments more she simply sat, naked with her face still streaked with tears, staring up at the window, the keys clenched in her hand. At last, she stood, hope soaring like a bird though she tried vainly to quash it down. Slowly, slowly, she walked to the window. She peered at the little lock, a small circle set neatly into the molding, barely visible. Even on tiptoe, she couldn't reach it. She remembered that Brenda had used a stepladder. But that ladder wasn't here. Brenda brought it in with her when she was going to secure Jane to chains hanging from the ceiling for some new and horrible torture.

What could she use? She scanned the room, her mind in a fever. Nothing here! They took it all away with them. Nothing but her cage. Her cage. Surely it was moveable? She had never tried to move it! But why not? How heavy could it be? Just bars and blankets? She could climb on it. What if they came home? What if they found her climbing on her cage to her window? She would be tortured within an inch of her life! Fear kept her still for some minutes more. She was so used to their constant presence, to the constant surveillance of the camera and the little microphones she had found hidden about the room. She still couldn't quite grasp that they might truly be gone! And so sure of themselves and her captivity that they let her know they would be gone!

She *must* try it. She must, or she was damming herself to a life of bondage and hopelessness. A life that would surely end in murder when they tired of her, and she never knew when that day might come. Screwing her courage to the sticking point, Jane began to push her cage across the floor. It moved rather easily, to her delight, though it scraped and scratched along the wood, making a terrible sound. Her heart pounding high in her throat, she continued until it was under her window. Even now these keys might not work, and her effort would have been in vain. But not to have tried would have been to give up. And Jane wasn't about to give up now.

She climbed up on the cage. The bars hurt her bare feet, but she hardly noticed, balancing so that she could get the little keys into the lock. The first one didn't fit and she almost cried with frustration. Again a whispered prayer. She inserted the second key and—

It fit.

She turned it slowly, feeling the lovely twist as the tumblers fell neatly into place. With trembling hands she pushed at the window. Smoothly it lifted, and a delicious breeze wafted in, blowing her hair gently from her face. The air was hot on this summer evening, but to Jane it felt like heaven. Freedom lay so close, like a promise; like a dream. If she could manage to get through this little window, she could escape! She had other keys. One of them was a car key. If she could get into the house, get some clothes, get into the garage. It was all so preposterous, so unlikely, that if she had taken a second to reason with herself, she would have been too daunted to attempt it. Luckily, she wasn't thinking at all now. She was only acting. She stuffed the keys into her mouth; the only safe place on her naked body while she carefully fit her head through the opening. Good. Her head fit with room the spare. Now her shoulders. If she could get them through she could get the rest of her body through as well. For once she was glad of her thin, scrawny frame.

Carefully she put one shoulder through, twisting to make herself narrower, and then the other. She was halfway out the window now. She was going to make it! She was going to escape! She fell with an ungraceful plop onto the soft lawn below, the keys jangling against her teeth. For a moment she was afraid she had sprained an ankle, but after a minute she felt all right. Just a little twist. She stood carefully, clutching the keys now in her hand, eyes darting, looking to see who was looking at her. What she saw was lush rolling lawn, which melted down a slope into a forest of trees. There was no one about. This must be the back of the house. She walked along the wall, staying close to it, looking for a door. She found one and tried the various door keys again. Luck was still with her as she opened what turned out to be the kitchen door.

She was in the house. She waited a moment, certain that an alarm would go off. The police would come and free her. Or arrest her, she realized. As a trespasser and burglar, charged with breaking and entering! A crazy naked woman with a bizarre story about being held prisoner by these millionaires who weren't even home. She could see it now, as they hauled her down to the station in handcuffs. She would exchange one prison for another with bars of steel and no way out.

But no alarm sounded. In fact, Robert and Brenda's security was located on the perimeters of the property and they didn't even need to lock their doors; it was that secure. If Jane had known this she might have been a good deal calmer. As it was, she ran into the bedroom, looking desperately for clothing. Brenda was so much larger that she didn't know what she'd find that would do. Rifling through the racks, she finally pulled out a short sundress and put it on. It wasn't too bad, though a little long for her. The soft fabric felt strange against flesh that had been kept naked for so many weeks. She grabbed a sash to use as a belt. She found some sandals in the closet that would stay on if she buckled them tight enough.

Then she saw it. The lovely ruby diamond bracelet, just sitting there! She ran to it and grabbed it. Brenda owed her this and much, much more, for stealing her life, for using her for all these weeks and months. Jane slipped it over her own thin wrist. It sparkled and felt wonderfully heavy. She would have time later to admire it, she hoped. For now, what else could she take? She would need money. She could never go back to her little apartment, the address of which had been neatly typed on the driver's license in the purse they had stolen from her. There was no home there any longer, surely. Her landlord would have gotten rid of all her things, written her off as another freeloader who had flown the coop.

Ah, if only she could find her purse! Have some identification.

No real time to look. She did a quick search in their huge closet, but didn't see her clothes or purse. They had probably disposed of it all long ago. She did grab one of Brenda's many bags. A nice leather one, large. Going back to the vanity, she scooped more jewelry into it. She opened the drawers, looking for something else of value, something easily convertible to cash. Nothing.

She went to the other bureau. Robert's, she assumed. On a little pewter tray lay a neat little stack of business cards. She picked one up and read, ROBERT CASSIDY—INVESTMENTS, with his address and phone number in small letters below it. For some reason she took one and slipped it into the pocket of her dress.

In the first drawer, she rifled through his underwear and socks. And then she felt it. A wad of cash held in a money clip. She pulled it out, hardly believing her luck. There were fifties and one hundred dollar bills! There had to be over a thousand dollars here! Jesus! Petty cash to these motherfuckers, but a fortune to Jane. A fortune that would buy her a plane ticket out of here. Then she could sell the jewelry at her leisure and begin her new life somewhere far, far away.

She stuffed the cash in the bag and ran from the room. Still clutching the keys tightly in a sweaty palm, she ran back to the kitchen, and through it to the garage. Four cars sat pristinely; the fifth space empty. The Lexus in which they had abducted her was nowhere to be seen. She looked down at her car key. It looked foreign. She knew nothing about cars, but went to the first one and opened it. She inserted the key. It didn't fit. She went to the next. It did. The engine started like a charm. She pushed the little button on the box secured to the visor and the garage door purred open.

She almost pulled out then and drove away, but something stopped her. Part of her screamed to get out of there, fast! But the stubborn part of her, the same one who had stuck with the wobbly cart, said *wait*. She wasn't quite done here. She wanted to leave them a present. She wanted to get them back just a little for stealing her life for all these weeks. Her precious, precious life. She climbed out of the car, leaving it idling, and looked quickly around the garage until she found what she was looking for. Gasoline. In a five gallon container of bright red plastic, with a handy nozzle for dispensing. She ran back into the house and began pouring the gas in the kitchen, in the living room, in the bedroom, a trail of destruction. She rummaged feverishly in the kitchen drawers until she found the matchbox. Striking three at once, she threw them on the gasoline and was gratified with a whoosh of sound as the gas lit and she saw the trail of fire work its way into the living room.

This time Jane didn't stick around to see if it caught. She ran back to the car, leaped in, and backed carefully out, turning around in the large drive and heading down to the gates. They opened on cue as sensors responded to her approaching car. She slid out and drove slowly, her foot shaking against the pedal as she tried to stay calm. She felt the little stiff business card poking against her thigh as she shifted in the seat. Some day she would use that card. She would call the police, once she was far away from here. Surely she wasn't the first person they had abducted and tortured and she probably wouldn't be the last. A well timed tip could put those two behind bars for life.

But now she focused on the road, looking for a sign to lead her to a main thoroughfare. Impulsively, she let out a whoop of sheer joy. She was doing it! She was reclaiming a life she was only now going to live. As she turned onto the public road, she fancied she saw the orange lick of a flame kissing the mansion behind her. She turned her eyes back to the road ahead, where freedom lay.

FIN